DEAD BY SATURDAY

Borgo Press Books by S. Fowler Wright

DEAD BY SATURDAY

AN INSPECTOR CLEVELAND CLASSIC CRIME NOVEL

by

S. FOWLER WRIGHT

WRITING AS "SYDNEY FOWLER"

THE BORGO PRESS

An Imprint of Wildside Press LLC

MMIX

CONTENTS

DEAD BY SATURDAY

CHAPTER I.

BASIL THORNFORD sat in the New Oxford Street tea-shop which faced the slanting junction of Shaftesbury Avenue, and defied the world with a light heart.

He had quarrelled with his only living relative in London about half an hour ago, he had £43 6s. 7d. in his pocket (he had just counted that, with some satisfaction), and he was sitting with his back to the wall, at a table which was otherwise solitary—a position which gave him a pleasant imagination of security and isolation, as he looked at the assorted sprinkling of office denizens who were fortifying themselves with glasses of hot milk and cups of coffee around him.

He had come up to London three weeks ago, leaving a guardian who very surely did not desire to see him again, to join a brother fifteen years older than himself, who considered the relationship justified him in the imposition of longer hours and the disbursing of smaller remunerations than were endured or received by any other members of his crowded office. But Basil Thornford had differed.

Devereux was a good business man, and it had not been good business to drive his brother too hard. But he had been ignorant of one vital fact, which no one had been allowed to know. That was the £50 which Basil had won as a fifth share in a crossword prize in *Tuckworth's Journal* two months ago. No one had been allowed to know of that £50, except the Pickston grocer who had obliged him by cashing the cheque.

Having the amount in your pocket, is it likely that you would listen patiently to a brother who tells you that he will give you five shillings a week for the first year (besides buying your clothes), and after that—well, we will see how you go on?

Five shillings is a small sum. You can't save much out of that. And, if you were twenty-one last month, you will agree that a year is a long time.

Why, if he saved two-and-sixpence a week, he would scarcely replace the £6 13s. 5d. which he had already spent from his original capital! Not much Dick Whittington business about that.

Besides, there was the way Devereux laughed. Even the quarrel this morning had seemed like a joke to him. No doubt he thought he would find him at home when he got back this afternoon—in his car. And the programme had been that Basil should follow about two hours later—by bus.

"If you think you can get a better job, you'd better try." That had been what he had said, and Basil had replied, "That's the first thing we've agreed about since I came here." And then he had laid down the letter which he had been told to take to Furnival Street and wait for a reply, picked up his hat and walked out. And so here he was. It would have happened a week ago, only that he had had an idea. Supposing he went on for six months, or even twelve, and studied the business intensely during that period? Might he not then open in opposition, and by superior foresight and organizing capacity so capture and control the trade, that in two or three years (if not less) he would be magnanimously taking over the Dickinson & Thornford firm? In imagination, he had written cheques for Devereux's creditors with a liberal hand. He had even given him a place in his own firm, not at five shillings a week, but at a figure sufficient (if he were careful) to keep on the comfortable villa where he now resided, and in which Basil had received the hospitality of an attic room. He wouldn't want Devereux to be turned out of that. Not Ethel, anyway. He rather liked his brother's wife. Which was natural enough, as she liked him. But, all the same, Devereux would have to be careful if he went on living there. He was rather fond of discoursing on the importance of being careful with money. So let him try it himself.

But he had rejected this project. He applied the appropriate lines of the Rev. F. H. C. Doyle's poem to the wisdom and moral courage which he had displayed in this decision.

> ...with strength like steel
> He put the vision by.

He had considered the inadequacy of his available capital, even when augmented by such sums as could be saved out of five shillings a week. He had observed that the business of an East India merchant requires a more substantial capital, if it is to be conducted on liberal lines. The rejection of this alluring dream showed the

clear-sighted judgment which made his ultimate success such an obvious thing.

And as he had drunk his coffee, and gazed reflectively upon the
moving crowd, he had seen the adventure of life which was before
him, in all its glory. He sat there solitary, unknown. So he would
remain. Predatory, hawk-like, taking tribute from the wealth of the
unsuspecting city. He knew that criminals usually work in gangs,
and are betrayed by their associates. Besides, they are known to the
police. They are so frequently men of low character, easy to separate
from the more respectable fellows. Too often, they do sordid, despi-
cable things, rather than those that are splendid and spectacular.
They may be urged to such courses by actual want, whereas he was
independent, through the capital he possessed. He could look round
at a serene and isolated leisure, deciding where he should swoop.
What, for instance, about robbing a bank? There could be no real
harm in that. But there would be no hasty decisions with him. He
must look round. And, first of all, he must remove his personal possessions from 46, Western Road before Devereux got back. There
was no use in having another wrangle with him.

As he concluded these reflections, and prepared to leave, he observed that a young woman of some physical attractions had seated
herself at his table. He picked up a check that was near his cup, and
she interposed to say in a rather pleasant voice: "I think that's mine,
isn't it?"

So, on examination, it proved to be. His own had fallen on to
the floor. He thanked her briefly for the correction, as he rose to go.
But he was not going to be drawn into so dangerous a conversation.
He knew better than that. What are the words of François Villon?

Good luck has he that deals with none!

You cannot be too careful to avoid female entanglements when
you are about to adventure upon a life of crime.

CHAPTER II.

BASIL walked to the end of Tottenham Court Road, looked round in what he felt to be a satisfactorily predatory manner, as an invader may gaze upon a captured city, which he will sack at his own convenience. Then he mounted the Richmond bus.

A life of crime cannot be commenced too soon. Well aware that the distance that he proposed to travel required a nine-penny fare, he boldly purchased a six-penny ticket. At Hammersmith, an inspector boarded the bus. Was his first experiment to end in failure? No, he remembered with satisfaction that his ticket was still in order for the distance covered. It was even returned to him politely, and when he left the bus, twenty minutes later, he was able to congratulate himself upon the result of his first adventure. He had successfully withheld three pence from the hands of the spoiler. He felt that a shilling honestly earned would have given him an inferior pleasure. It was worth even the somewhat uncomfortable feeling he had had during the last quarter of an hour of the journey, when the conductor had paraded between the seats calling out *Fares please. Any more fares?* in what had sounded to him a very suspectful voice. Wouldn't it be a good plan to put the three pence aside? To begin to accumulate the results of successful criminalities, to see how much could be gathered before his present capital disappeared? Realizing the soundness of this plan, he transferred the amount to his hip-pocket.

These reflections occupied him during the short walk that took him to the door of his brother's house. Here he must ring, for the fraternal tyranny had withheld the latch-key for which he had asked. He did hope Ethel wouldn't make any scene! Suppose she telephoned to Devereux, and they tried to stop him going away? Of course they could not do that. He was old enough to please himself. Yet he felt a natural relief when the maid said that Mrs. Thornford was out—and would he like any lunch?

He decided that he certainly would. He had a very healthy appetite. And, besides, was it not rather in the style of spoiling the Philistine and the Egyptian to lunch thus at his brother's table after he had repudiated him and his a couple of hours ago?

Well, perhaps hardly that, considering he had done more than two days' work for which he was unpaid. And now he would have to pay for the next meal. Thinking of this melancholy fact, he ate well.

It did not take him long to pack his clothes, and the few books that were his. They filled two rather large suitcases, and the books made them heavy. Still, he could carry them a short way, if he must.

He got downstairs without bumping the suitcases very loudly, and Irene, who was washing up in the basement, continued to sing, *It Will Be Glory for Me* in undisturbed serenity. It was a song of which she was fond, and it could only be rendered with a full voice when her mistress had gone to town. Such opportunities should not be lost in listening, simply because Mr. Basil was moving about the house.

He went into the lounge to get the fountain pen that he had left there rather carelessly the night before, and noticed a little pile of silver and copper on the mantelpiece. He realized that a criminal of the baser sort would have picked it up, but he would levy toll in lordlier ways than that. Not Ethel's housekeeping money, anyway. But he remembered the two days' salary (not counting the morning) which was due to himself. That would be one and eight pence— counting the same amount for Saturday as though it were a full day. He took this, leaving a little note under the pile:

DEAR ETHEL,

I've taken one and eight pence that Devereux owes me. I suppose he won't be mean enough not to give it you back.

Good-bye,

BASIL

That would show them his magnanimity, alone with the whole sum in his power, and having scorned to take advantage of opportunity.

Ethel did not think of it in that way when she read the note, not being aware that he had embarked upon a life of crime. But she actually cried at the thought of him, penniless and alone in the London streets. How far would one and eight pence go? Such is the folly of women.

CHAPTER III.

BASIL walked down the quiet suburban road, feeling the weight of his personal property to be somewhat excessive—even without the underclothing that had gone to the wash, which must be regarded as lost for ever. It was early summer, and quite warm in the afternoon; and the worst of having two suitcases of about equal weight is that you can't change hands. Not to do any good that is. And you don't want to lay them down in the road looking a fool, and not knowing whether Ethel's taxi may pass you at any moment, and she seeing you more likely than not. Ethel didn't miss much. No, it was better to hurry on to the end of the road, and get to where you might find a taxi yourself.

When he did succeed in hailing a vacant vehicle, he was somewhat hot and dishevelled and bad-tempered, but he had formed his plans with great subtlety while he had had lunch, and he now said, without hesitation, "Isleworth, please," and asked to be put down at the tea-shop just beyond the *Rose and Crown*. And so he sat there for the best part of an hour, getting up what appetite he could while his lunch slowly receded into the past, and considering what name he should take. He knew that it is a common error among money-lenders and other criminals to adopt names of an impressive unreality, such as Fortescue Plantagenet, or Percival Montmorency, but he knew better than that. "John Williams" would be a better choice. It would be easier to believe in a name like that. Not the kind that anyone would be likely to choose, unless it were closely related to him. John Williams it should be.

The bus stopped almost opposite, on the other side of the road. He took a ticket to Gower Street without attempting an illicit deduction. He told himself that it would be too conspicuous to the conductor (he having two suitcases under his care) to make it worth trying. His forbearance showed the skill of the master criminal.

At 5:00 P.M. John Williams had taken a bed-sitting room (third-floor back) for a pound a week, and the landlady had so far failed to

15

read his true character by his face, that she had actually refrained from asking for the deposit which she required from the more volatile of her ever-changing guests.

Reflecting on this omission, he realized with a natural satisfaction how well he had been equipped by nature for the profession in which he had resolved to qualify.

He did not go out again that evening, being fully occupied in unpacking and distributing his possessions, and in the further and somewhat difficult negotiations with the landlady which followed his belated recognition of the fact that he had made no bargain in respect of attendance, or the provision or cooking of meals. He found Mrs. Postler to be coy of figures under these headings. She professed lack of experience. She said that most of the guests "does for theirselves in their own rooms." But the passage of a ten-shilling note for the provision of bread and cheese and bacon and newly-laid eggs assisted her imagination to the point of agreeing upon experimental terms for the first week, after which she said vaguely that they must see how they got on.

This payment reduced the capital of John Williams *contra mundum* to £42 12s. 4d., apart from the three pennies isolated in his hip-pocket. He considered the safeguarding of this capital with some anxiety. A bank would have been the obvious resort, but in what name should he approach such an institution? It might be awkward for John Williams to have to sign a cheque as Basil Thornford. As to John Williams—suppose he should deposit his money in that name, and find an unexpected difficulty in getting it back? Suppose he forgot just how he had signed, and the bank asked him to prove his identity? It would be extremely difficult to produce living or documentary witnesses who could establish him in that name. No; the identity of John Williams was of too tender an infancy to be subjected to such an experience. Give it time to grow.

Besides, was it not more consistent with the profession of banditry which he had adopted to guard that which was his with his own arm or his own wit rather than to rely upon the protection of those upon whom he was to wage a plundering war? Was there not even some lack of chivalry in accepting such assistance from them? No, he would be his own guardian, both of the fortune which was his already, and that which he was about to win.

But to carry it with him on all his enterprises was a risk which should be avoided, if possible. He looked round for a safe hiding-place. His reading told him that the floor ought to have a loose board. Perhaps it had, but as it was completely covered with a nailed-down carpet it was not easy to reach.

He might push a few one-pound notes under the carpet, but, in the highly unlikely event of Mrs. Postler having it up in his absence for cleaning purposes, there might be difficulty in convincing her that it was his property that had come into her possession. It might be even more hazardous to go out after informing her of where he had deposited them. Such are the worries that only the wealthy know.

Finding no other solution to the problem, he decided to carry his capital in his pocket until some change of circumstances should relieve his difficulties. If possible, he would exchange it into a less bulky form. In the end, he put twenty pounds into the wallet in his breast-pocket, and distributed the remainder into other pockets in a spirit of caution on which he had occasion to congratulate himself a few days later, and which confirmed the cool, impartial self-judgment which recognized, and had the honesty to admit, the Napoleonic qualities which fitted him for the enterprise he had undertaken.

Four days later, he was seated at breakfast, eating the stale egg which Mrs. Postler had provided, and occupied with reflections which had less than his usual mental resilience.

In the first place, his hip-pocket still contained no more than three pennies. He had resolved that thought should precede action, and there would have been no occasion for worrying over this short period, if it had not passed without supplying him with any satisfactory plan of campaign for the days to follow.

He had declared war upon the organized wealth and power of the unregarding community around him, which is a very exhilarating thing to do, but the concentrated thought of three days had suggested no more fruitful and profitable method of attack than the popular sport of shop-lifting, to which he felt an almost invincible disinclination. This was not, he assured himself, because of any fear of the risk to his own liberty which it implied, nor any doubt of his capacity to operate successfully, because, should he decide upon it, he would give it the Napoleonic consideration which it required. Neither was it because the profession of shop-lifting is almost a monopoly of the female half of the community. Why should he not demonstrate once again, as has been done in other feminine domains, such as cooking or dress-designing, the superiority of the male?

No. It was rather that it had an aspect of retail pettiness. It was almost—dishonest. He had no love of dishonesty. But to sack a city is not dishonest. Under suitable circumstances, it is as natural as to tax it. It is the question of broad vision. What had Lord Tennyson to say on the subject?

> Believe me, private and public war
> Are scarcely even akin.

Without crediting Alfred Tennyson with sufficient enterprise to have faced the world as he was now doing, he realized the soundness of that assurance, and believed him without difficulty.

But when he looked to them for any concrete suggestions, the poets were less helpful. They might enunciate

> ...the simple plan
> That he should take who has the power,
> And he should keep who can.

(even Wordsworth, of all people!) with great cheerfulness; but when you looked to them for any concrete suggestions—well, they simply weren't there.

Yesterday his predatory wanderings had taken him round the Caledonian market.

He had seized no prey, but he had conducted a prosaic commercial transaction by which he had acquired a very antiquated copy of *Every Man's Own Lawyer* for five pence.

He had considered reasonably that the age of the book would not substantially reduce its value to him. Its laws might be obsolescent, but its catalogue of crimes would remain as suggestive as on its day of publication.

It had proved a disappointing book. It was not only its exposure of the fact that most of the warfare which the individual makes on the community is of an utterly unprofitable kind, with no possible issue but his own undoing. Worse than that was the realization that there were so few crimes which it was in his power to commit.

How could he commit bigamy? How could he sell meat after hours? How could he fail to keep a poison register, or succeed in keeping a manservant without a licence? How could he purloin a locomotive, which is expressly forbidden by the bylaws of the Great Western Railway Co., with a penalty of £5 for the first offence, and much heavier liabilities for anyone who persists in collecting these curios?

It was theoretically possible for him to commit a criminal assault upon the somewhat austere female who occupied the room on the other side of the landing, but in practice (and particularly after the way in which she had snubbed him yesterday) he knew that it could not be. He would be far too shy.

What remained? Could he break a lease? Could he leave his children to the public charge? Could he move cattle without a licence into an infected area? Could he issue base coin, not knowing where they were to be obtained?

It remained that he could commit murder, or retail theft, or send explosives by post. A poor choice.

He learnt that there are penalties provided also for those who fail to commit suicide, but there was no consolation in that. He did not want to fail in anything that he undertook, even with the satisfaction of knowing that it was illegal to do so.

So he wandered out disconsolately, and in the window of a little shop in a back street in Clerkenwell he noticed a half-filled stamp-album, which he purchased for 5s., and took it to a dealer in the Strand, who gave him 32s. for it, after they had talked for an hour, and soaked off some of the stamps.

He sat in a tea-shop for some time after that, suffering from a natural depression. Was he being driven, by powers which he could not rule, back to all the monotonies of those who make their livings in conventional ways? It was a bitter thought, and yet, if in three days he had only made three pence by nefarious means, and £1 7s. by legitimate barter, what must the deduction be?

And yet, what is three days?

He wandered back into New Oxford Street, surveying the shop windows and the moving crowds with a pleasant sense of ownership, such as a young wolf may feel as he surveys the feeding flock from the wood's edge. He may never have caught one yet, but there is the pleasant consciousness that they are his destined prey. As he approached Charing Cross Road, he noticed a shop which had been temporarily occupied by one of those travelling auctioneers who present gold watches and rings to the public with a generosity which cannot be expected to continue long in one locality. Must not others benefit also?

The floor of the shop was a cleared space, with a rostrum at its further end. It was crowded with spectators, mostly of the idly curious kind, but doubtless containing also the necessary percentage of fools, by whom the entertainment would be financed. The experienced eye of the auctioneer searched the crowd unwinkingly for his appropriate prey, while his mouth continued to pour out the glib audacities by which he mesmerized them to the folly which would seem so inexplicable when they got outside, with ten shillings gone from their pockets and a sixpenny parcel of something they did not want under their arms.

John Williams was aware that the auctioneer was looking upon him in a respectful and admiring way. "Show it to that gentleman on the right," he shouted to the assistant who was carrying round a very gaudy clock (positively one of the very last three) which were to be given away practically for nothing as an incentive to a good Saturday afternoon's trade.

John Williams shook his head. He had no use for a clock. Faced by the noxious article, he reluctantly consented to handle it. He said, "Very nice, I'm sure," as he laid it back on the tray.

As he did so, he noticed a hostile glance which the attendant gave to a slim, sandy-haired youth with a rather furtive manner who was pressing against his side, perhaps even more closely than was necessitated by the crowd round them. He heard, "Here, clear out, we don't want your sort here," spoken in a low voice. Doubtless the auctioneer felt that he could abstract all the spare money from his audience that they could afford to lose without the competition of the cruder practitioner. The attendant seeing that he was not yet sufficiently mesmerized for a bid, passed on to the charming of riper prey.

It was a couple of minutes later that there was a sudden pressure around him. The crowd seemed to be bearing on him from two sides at once. Turning in his effort to free himself, he saw the sandy head of the youth whom he had heard the attendant warn, very close behind him. With an instinctive caution his hand went to his breast pocket, as it did a good many times during the day. But this time the result was less satisfactory than usual. The wallet was not there. Neither, when he looked again, was the sandy head. A dreadful fear was in the heart of John Williams, but the Napoleonic brain continued to function. He connected the two disappearances instantly, and in the same instant he was elbowing his way to the door. He reached it just in time to see the youth mixing with the pavement crowd, and pursued him at the quick walk which he had himself adopted. Complicating the angry determination to recover his property, he was already conscious of some doubt of how to proceed. His plans had been made entirely to suit his new profession. He was to be what a lawyer might describe as a crimor. He had not anticipated the less satisfactory position of the crimee.

Suppose he were to seize the young man by the arm and demand his property. He supposed that a denial would naturally follow. What then? Should he give him in charge? And, if so, by what name? From what address? How should he prove that the money was his?

Anyway, he must have a try. He quickened his pace further, and was almost upon his prey when the sandy head turned. Their eyes met. The youth ran.

Naturally, Basil followed. He had the better legs of the two, and the chase would have been a short one on a clear course. But the thief dodged through the traffic, and slanted leftward up Hart Street. Basil, trying to follow a moment later, found the swift rush of vehicles had become too dense for immediate passage. When he got over, at some risk to himself, he was only able to follow in time to see the youth turn in at the side of St. George's Church. But he had put on such speed, with the thought of that £20, the theft of which had been practically admitted by the flight, that he caught sight of him again as he followed along the passage at the left hand of the Church.

Where the passage turns at the back of the church, there is a short flight of steps, and a gate, which is open in the day, as the youth doubtless knew, beyond which is a railed-in yard, and an exit to Little Russell Street. Just beyond the steps there is another short flight which descends to a detached Vestry Hall, and down these steps the youth threw something as he passed, which Basil, now close at his heels, supposed to be the wallet which had been taken from him.

The device, which is as old as Atalanta (and doubtless older), had its usual result. Basil ran down the half-dozen steps instead of continuing the pursuit to a certain capture. He picked up a heavy pocket-case larger and much better filled than his own.

Seeing that it was not his, he pushed it hastily into his pocket and resumed the chase. But the minute gained had been well used. The short length of Little Russell Street was bare between the crossings of the two side streets that lead to the British Museum. He might have gone either way. Basil ran to the right, and a boy, kicking his heels against the wall, pointed him backward with a grin. He ran into Coptic Street, but he knew as he did it that the pursuit had failed.

His twenty pounds was gone, but what had he got in its place? He must find a quiet locality for its examination. It did not require exceptional intelligence to divine that it had been stolen, like his own. To examine it in public might be a dangerous thing to do. If the owner should stroll along, or a suspicious constable ask him to explain his possession, it might not be easy.

Prudence counselled that he should defer examination till he should be in the solitude of his own room. Gower Street was close at hand. He restrained his curiosity while he walked there at a brisk pace.

CHAPTER IV.

TWENTY minutes later, John Williams was packing his suit-case in frantic preparation for an instant flight. He had had one astonished glance at the contents of the pocket-case, one sudden memory of the misguided caution which had caused him to insert a card that morning into the stolen wallet—a card that had stated that it was the property of John Williams of 26B Gower Street, N.W.1—and his resolution was taken.

As he entered, he had met Mrs. Postler going out with a string bag on her arm. Doubtless, she had the weekend shopping on her hands. She would be gone for an hour. Before then he would have fled from her roof for ever. It had become an unavoidable incident of the situation that he should leave without the formality of notice, or requesting her to present her bill. He might, after fuller consideration, have decided to leave some silver on the table as an approximately accurate offering, but he remembered the profession of criminality which he had undertaken. He had no time for the debating of moral problems. He hardened his heart with a recollection of the stale eggs which had been laid before him. He confirmed his judgment with the memory of how easily he had left his brother's house at about the same hour of the day. The essential thing was to be gone—to be gone somewhere beyond the possibility of pursuit. Somewhere where he could think in peace.

Ten minutes later, his two suitcases were deposited beside the conductor of a Hampstead bus.

Having recovered his breath from their rapid haulage clear of the dangerous vicinity of Gower Street, and having time for cooler reflection as the bus proceeded northward, he considered that it was improbable that he had anything to fear (at least immediately) from police pursuit. He decided that the thief must either have thrown the pocketbook away in mistake for his own or he must have abstracted it from its owner too recently to have had any opportunity of investigating its contents. But, even so, when he saw the reward which would be offered (surely that was a certainty!), would he not immediately get on the track of John Williams, to whom he had thrown it, whose address had been so obligingly supplied in his own wallet? Well, perhaps not. Looking at it coolly, even if he saw the offer of the reward, and should connect it with the pocketbook that he had thrown away, he might hesitate to venture on a call upon the man he had robbed, though he might arrange for others to do so. More probable, and more imminent, was the danger that he had been aware of the contents of that which he had thrown away in a panic error. Would he not risk everything for its recovery?

No, perhaps not even then. As he got cooler, he began to see that his first impulse might have exaggerated the importance of a speedy flight. And yet—no, the sooner the better. He could not have stayed there without continued fear. A reward might even be announced in the evening papers. What should prevent the thief going to the police, and saying, "I saw it stolen by a man named Williams. This is his address. Seize him quickly, and the reward will be mine!" Living under an assumed name, without honest occupation, found in possession of such a prize, what credible defence could he hope to make? No, he was best away.

He walked some distance from the bus, down a drab side-street where scores of small bow-windowed houses were repeated in two monotonous rows. Many of them displayed window-cards offering "apartments" to be let, and at one of these, which looked somewhat cleaner than its competitors, he stopped, and quickly acquired the first-floor front from a vacuous-faced woman for eighteen and sixpence a week, payable in advance in lieu of references, which she evidently considered a more than satisfactory alternative.

He gave the name of "Percy Rogers," and said that he was a traveller in the motor trade, but had just been engaged by new employers who would not require him to take up his duties till the first of the coming month. That was a precaution, in case he should not want to be seen abroad during the next few days.

The woman inquired whether he would like a meal, and received an emphatic affirmative. Meals would be extra. Of course. He understood that? Yes, that was quite clear. With cheerful celerity she laid the table, and offered him the luxury of a stale egg.

CHAPTER V.

WITH a self-control which he assured himself was more Napoleonic even than the high standard of his general conduct, he forbore a fuller examination of the pocketbook, of which he had as yet had no more than one bewildering glimpse, until he had eaten the meal, and it had been cleared away.

It was not only that he must lock the door. He wished to do it when he could be reasonably sure that he would be undisturbed. He might wish to keep it locked for some considerable time, and he did not wish to do anything which would draw the attention of Miss Sporethought (at least, that was what her name had sounded like to him: it was probably wrong) to any singularity in his conduct. Who knew what might be in the newspapers on Monday morning? Suppose she should knock at the door while he had the contents scattered on the table, and he must decline to open? She might look through the key-hole!

That, at least, he would prevent. What fortune that there was a key in the door! He would hang a handkerchief over it.

He went to the door with this satisfactory intention, and found a preliminary and unexpected difficult. The key would not turn. At least, it would not do so when the door was shut. A short consideration of this dilemma showed him that it was beyond remedy unless the door should be rehung, or the slot in the jamb be enlarged. The latter was the more promising method, but there was a metal plate to be removed, for which a screw-driver was a necessity

He considered that the most impecunious or innocent of lodgers may desire to sleep in a room which can be locked at night, or to leave his humble possessions secure from promiscuous intrusion when he goes out in the day. He summoned Miss Sporethought to his assistance, and laid the problem before her.

She responded to his diffident protest with an interest which was friendly but aloof. She assured him that she hadn't knowed it to be like that, and that Mr. Latkins had been accustomed to put a chair under the handle when he was dressing, which was a needless precaution, she being one as would always knock if it was a gentleman's room. As to a screwdriver, she didn't rightly know. After which, she retired to the basement, and fetched a coal-hammer.

Percy Rogers said that it didn't matter at all.

The lady having withdrawn, Percy put the chair into the required position, draped his handkerchief over handle and key, satisfied himself that the window was sufficiently protected from the observation of anyone in the bedrooms on the opposite side of the road, and drew the pocketbook from his hip pocket.

It was of such bulk that it came out with difficulty, bringing the lining with it. Being opened, it displayed two major pockets, both fully stuffed, the one with paper money, and the other with miscellaneous documents. It did not appear probable that, with such a mass of material, there would be any difficulty in identifying its owner, and Percy Rogers may have shown how rapidly he was graduating in criminality when he commenced his investigation by emptying the paper money upon the table rather than directing his attention to the other pockets. But even that had some unusual features, such as would have enabled the average detective of fiction to deduce the appearance and character, if not the absolute identity of its owner, in the minutest detail.

First, there were six banknotes, neatly and flatly folded together. Four of them were for £1,000 each, and the remaining two were of half that value.

Percy noticed that the four £1,000 notes were numbered consecutively, as were the two others. They were uncreased, except for their present folding. It was a simple deduction that they had come straight from a bank, and that they represented a single transaction.

Second, there were nine banknotes of various denominations, from five pounds to fifty, some clean, some soiled, and one of twenty pounds being very dirty and badly torn at one corner, amounting to a total of £270.

Third, there was a U.S.A. thousand-dollar bill, and another for twenty-five.

Fourth, there was a banknote for £100, with five £1 notes folded inside it. "C.V.'s com. 18th" was pencilled on the outside of the note.

Besides these evidently allocated notes, there were no pound or ten-shilling notes there. Evidently, the owner of the pocketbook kept his petty cash loose in his pocket.

Percy Rogers added this wealth, making a total of £5,375 in English money, and something over £200 in that of the United States of America.

It was a comfortingly substantial sum. Sufficient to enable him to endure the thought of the £20 he had lost without any very unpleasant sensations, but he was not ignorant of the fact that banknotes are easy to trace, and may be very difficult to negotiate. Banknotes of £1,000 might be almost impossible for a young man whose name was only acquired during the afternoon. He remembered reading something about a white elephant. To negotiate them so that he could obtain their value without his own detection might be an impossible thing to attempt. To put them aside perhaps for many years, until a propitious opportunity should occur, might be the only prudent course if he should decide to retain that which had, almost literally, been thrown into his lap.

But there was the prospect of a reward being offered. Indeed, was it not rather a certainty, with such a sum at stake? Might it not be a case in which honesty would be actually the most profitable policy to pursue? But if the identity of the owner should become evident from the contents of the second pocket, as he expected to find, would not he be criminally liable for its detention, if he waited for such a development. The thought naturally led him to resume his investigations.

CHAPTER VI.

IT was late when Percy Rogers went to bed, and even then he found sleep to be an impossible thing. He was so far relieved in mind that he felt clear of any responsibility for failing to communicate with the owner of the property which had come so strangely into his possession.

He had examined the whole of the documents with care, and they showed neither the owner's name nor any address which could be connected with him. They gave clues in plenty, but they were such as would need time and trouble to investigate, such as he could not be expected to undertake on Saturday night, nor, for that matter, on Sunday, either. Percy Rogers might be a man of particularly strict principles on the subject of Sabbath observance. He was not clear as to the extent of the legal obligation (if any) of a citizen making such a find to communicate it to the police, and there were several reasons why he would be reluctant to do so. Apart from that, he must await the announcement of a reward, when he would consider his position anew. The pocketbook had evidently belonged to some one of wide and varied interests, which was not surprising in view of the amount of cash which he carried about, but those interests appeared to be of a somewhat mysterious, and even sinister description.

Twice, in the midnight hours, Percy Rogers got out of bed, switched on the single electric light, and referred again to the papers which were scattered upon the table. In doing this he found fresh stimulus for the imagination, but little of a clearly informative character.

There were several slips of paper, bearing memoranda or messages which appeared to relate mainly to appointments, either past or future, and which were in different handwritings. There was *Ins. R. Corner H. St. Sth. 5:15 P.M. 17th.* "Ins." might be an Inspector or an Institution. It might mean something quite different. It would require a dictionary to exhaust its possibilities. The names of many streets in London commence with H. And this one might be in Bristol or Manchester!

There was *Belcher refuses unless double for Cox*. There were many people in London bearing one or other of those respectable names. They were the kind of memoranda which might be conclusive in proving the identity of an owner already found, but less useful at an earlier stage of inquiry. This one was in another hand from the others, and had the aspect of an anonymous message which the owner of the pocketbook had received.

There was a clue of another kind in a cheque on the Farmers' First National Bank of Nashville, Tennessee, for three thousand dollars, drawn to self by Silas T. Winger, payment of which had been refused. This cheque was dated May 13th, 1930, and folded up with it was a cutting from the *Tennessee Times* dated July 2nd, 1930, relating how the body of Silas Winger had been found, freely perforated with bullets, in his own yard.

The juxtaposition of these two documents might have no sinister significance, but Percy Rogers felt an excusable measure of doubt on this point as he lay awake in the night. The cheque drawn to himself by the unfortunate Mr. Winger, which had passed into other hands, and then been stopped by him, had too much of the suggestion of an illicit or blackmailing payment made under threats, or in a moment of weakness of which he afterwards repented. The shot-riddled body, too, seemed likely to represent an act of vengeance for that dishonoured cheque.

There were other papers which, when this idea had once taken root in his mind, appeared to be of a vaguely menacing character. Lists of names, or initials, amounts, and dates, giving an impression of far-reaching power, which was yet of such a nature that its documentary records must be by implication rather than by clear statement, even when they were in the possession of him by whom that power was controlled.

Of one thing Percy felt sure. The owner of that pocketbook was not a man who would accept his loss in a meekly Christian spirit. If he should call for it, Percy felt that he should much prefer to be out at the time.

But he was not destitute of courage. Since Tuesday morning, he had endeavoured vainly to graduate in the school of crime. If he were being introduced to it by a path which he had not sought, could he reasonably complain? He resolved to face the event confidently and, with a pleasant sense of adventure before him, he went to sleep at last.

CHAPTER VII.

THE next day, Percy Rogers remained indoors. He had no occupation except the furtive re-examination of the documentary contents of the stolen property which he had so innocently acquired, and the reading from his small library of poetry, in which he was unable to discover any passage really appropriate to his present situation, which was an unusual experience.

He became increasingly dissatisfied with the name which he had too hastily adopted yesterday. He considered with some relief that he had not yet mentioned it to anyone except Miss Sporethought, and he felt confident that she was not a lady of a very accurate memory. Beside that, he had gained an impression that she was rather deaf. And he comforted himself with the thought that, though his own hearing was good, he wasn't very sure of her own name.

He resolved at last that there could be no harm in destroying a name so young, so weak, that it might even be questioned whether it had arrived at the point of parturition from his own mind. You might call it stillborn.

At the same time, he did not wish to arouse any suspicion of the simple straightforwardness of his character. He had observed that Miss Sporethought had called him Mr. Rogers more than once already. He felt that, even if she were a little deaf, it would cause surprise if he were to say, "Pardon me, Miss Sporethought, I don't think you could have heard quite distinctly. My name isn't Rogers, it's Throckmorton"—or even Gillespie. No, it must really begin with R. How about Rodney? Not too startling. Not like Plantagenet. And yet manly. Quite a naval, adventurous sound. And he would return to the John of his first choice. Too many changes were confusing. You don't want to forget your own name. It isn't done.

"John Rodney"—of where? He felt the necessity for some background to the personality which he was about to create. Why not Plymouth? A naval town. He had visited it when he was six. Had actually stayed there for several months. It gave him a feeling of confidence, of familiarity, which he could not have felt in claiming the acquaintance of Middlesbrough or Barrow-in-Furness. And it had a Hoe. He could talk quite familiarly of the Hoe. The only trouble was that he had no idea what a Hoe is.

Perhaps Portsmouth would be better.

"All the way by Fratton tram, down to Portsmouth 'Ard."

That was a very apposite recollection. Who could doubt his acquaintance with Portsmouth when he talked familiarly of the Fratton tram?

At the laying of the evening meal he inquired timidly whether his landlady could oblige him with a sight of the newspaper which he had seen delivered with the morning milk. She met this request with so much cordiality that he was encouraged to announce the name which had been his since the previous midnight. She accepted the correction without displaying any unmannerly suspicion, and volunteered to lend him books, if he were short of reading, from her own resources, to which he replied with a suitable gratitude.

Miss Sporethought's library was inherited from very respectable Victorian ancestors. She examined it for such fare as she felt would be most suitable for a pleasant-mannered young gentleman whose name was Rogers one day and Rodney the next, but remained Thornford on his pyjamas, and produced *Little Meg's Children* and *The Swiss Family Robinson*. He had not read either of these books previously, and found the first to be of an absorbing interest, but the adventures in the tropic menagerie appeared to verge on the improbable in several places.

So the day passed, and the next morning came without any plan of action having been clearly determined.

Percy Rogers's inclination had been to remain in a safe seclusion while watching for the announcing of a reward of a sufficient magnitude. Perhaps a hundred pounds. Perhaps five. And the grateful owner could scarcely do less than recompense him for the twenty pounds which he had lost in so good a cause. It had been, as it were, the bait that had hooked the prey. Then there had been the equally necessary exhibition of John Williams's swift and fearless pursuit through the crowding perils of the New Oxford Street traffic. Yes, he could not hesitate over the twenty pounds. So Percy Rogers had thought. He had remembered a good phrase to describe his strategy. "Masterly inactivity." He was not sure whether he had read it somewhere or it had originated in his own mind, but anyway it was a good phrase. Far better than "Wait and see."

But John Rodney waked in a different mood. He remembered that "the best defence is attack" which is also a good phrase, and much more congenial to one who has been confined for about forty hours in a bed-sitting room of a dull and ugly complexion. He was quick to observe the disadvantages of immobility for a leader whose Intelligence Department has not been organized.

How was he to learn of the offered reward unless he should examine the output of the daily press? Miss Sporethought might be unable to observe the difference between Rogers and Rodney, but she could scarcely fail to conclude that she had given shelter to a fugitive criminal, if she should be asked to bring him in about thirty newspapers daily, while he remained in the voluntary confinement of his own room. Most probably, she would search the papers herself, and identify him with some desperate thief or coiner, and inform the police. Suppose he should be unable to prove that he was not the man they sought? The idea of a long term of imprisonment for some one else's crime was peculiarly distasteful. He seemed, somehow, to be graduating backwards in his new profession. Instead of committing crimes such as would place him high in the romanceful records of those who give battle to the coercions of their fellowmen, he felt himself to be drawing nearer to the grotesque humiliations of those who are accused of evils for which they have no responsibility—grotesque, that is, in such a case as his. He had thought to commit picturesque crime with sufficient enterprise and originality to escape the prosaic penalty: he felt himself to be in danger of the penalty, without having committed any crime at all.

Or at least—he supposed there was a certain amount of illegality in his abrupt departure from his Gower Street lodging, without the usual detail of a receipted bill. But, guilty or innocent, it would be all the same if he were apprehended with that pocketbook in his possession. His changes of name, to neither of which could he demonstrate any well-rooted attachment, and his sudden flight from Gower Street—he felt that there would be no more to be said!

But that was not all. He was not sure that it was the worst. He had a vision of the owner of that pocketbook as a man of violence and blood, now pursuing a vengeful search for the thief who had abstracted it from its natural home. He felt instinctively that he was a criminal like himself. At least, not *quite* like himself. Not a brilliant amateur, but a professional of a particularly brutal, greedy and unscrupulous kind. One whose enemies lay shot-riddled in the backyard. Being unfamiliar with the American language, he imagined the unfortunate Silas in a small brick-paved enclosure, lying beside the pump.

But John Rodney was undismayed. He felt some confidence that his retreat would not be discovered, some comfort in the size of London. He was of the temperament which is inspired by the call to action. He felt that it was indeed John Rodney *contra mundum*. The nautical associations of the name produced Dobell as the appropriate poet:

> But what is that to me?
> For the little *Betsy Jane* bobs to nothing on the sea.
> In she runs,
> And her guns
> Thunder round.

He hummed the defiant song to a tune of his own improvisation, while the fried haddock cooled on his plate. As he came to the last line, his plans were formed.

He would go straight to the Holborn Library, and make a thorough search of the daily papers for any record of the loss of the pocketbook in the news columns, or any offer of reward among the advertisements. After that—well, it must depend upon the result of that search. He did not omit to consider that he would be returning to the district in which he had met the thief, and where he might be likely to be encountered, if he were really seeking him. But he reflected also, with a soundness of judgment which gave some support to his own estimate of his Napoleonic potentialities, that he knew the way to the Holborn Library, and that he had no familiarity with any other public reading-room. It is those who look round, who loiter and hesitate, who are observed by others. Let him go straight to his purpose, and he would be secure from any probable observation among the crowds of the London streets.

But as he rose to go he became aware of another difficulty. Was he to carry about with him not only the residue of his own capital, but the large sum of which he had become the, say, custodian? Was he to leave it in the unlocked room?

Impatience for action led him to a quicker decision than he might otherwise have reached. He realized that banknotes for £500 and £1,000 are unlikely to attract the cupidity of the casual pilferer. They would be safer in the suitcase that had a lock of a sort—the other had none—than in his pocket, which had been picked once already. So—more doubtfully—might the American notes also. The smaller banknotes might be too tempting a lure for anyone who might explore his belongings while he was away. He distributed them among his numerous pockets, together with the money which was more legitimately his own. Even an expert pickpocket would have to work for a considerable time before he could completely rob him. Finally he endeavoured to insert the pocketbook in the hip-pocket in which he had carried it previously, and from which he had abstracted it with so much difficulty.

But the lining, which had been strained and torn on the last occasion, now refused to entertain such a proposition again, even though the contents had been somewhat diminished. The cracking sound which followed his impatient effort to force it down warned him that it could no longer be considered a safe, even if it were still a possible means of carrying it.

In fact, the pocketbook would have attempted the descent of his trouser leg much more readily than it would consent to be withdrawn through the aperture of the damaged pocket, and it was while he was struggling to overcome this difficulty that Miss Sporethought gave a perfunctory knock at the door, and entered to clear the table.

Very fortunately, though he could not have foreseen this, she observed sufficient of his gymnastics to have it firmly fixed in her mind that he was starting out with a black pocketbook of somewhat unusual bulk. As a fact, he left it behind, for after that experience he waited till she was going down with the tray, and deposited it in the suitcase with the major banknotes. He thought again, as he did this, how formidable must be the man in whose ample pocket it had doubtless dropped to a safe and roomy depth.

CHAPTER VIII.

JOHN RODNEY spent a long morning in the reading room of the Holborn Library. He had to make a detailed examination of about twenty possible newspapers, and his labours were appreciably prolonged by the development of a chronic indisposition to allow any other seeker of news to brush against or behind him. Considering his recent experience and the fact that he had several hundred pounds of paper money distributed over his person, we cannot blame him for his timidity, though the resulting inconvenience to himself and others was sufficient to cause one of the library assistants to observe him with a fixed suspicion as the morning advanced. He did not, fortunately, regard him as shifting his position with any criminal purpose, or he would have summoned a constable—and what would have happened subsequently can be a matter of conjecture only—but he considered that he was probably suffering from some disease of irritability, which might be of a contagious character, such as an eczema of a particularly malignant kind, and he was only restrained by constitutional timidity from requesting him to withdraw.

The result of this sensitiveness in a rather crowded room, and the intervals of waiting for such papers as were in use—intervals which increased in length as the list of those which he had still to inspect diminished—was that it was some hours before he was able to feel complete assurance that the owner of the stolen property was accepting his loss without any public outcry. To consider his position in the light of this knowledge, and to remedy an internal void which was becoming clamorous, he decided to cross the road to the tea-shop in which he had made the momentous resolution from which these adventures sprang.

In this decision, he remembered his purpose not to hesitate or loiter in the streets, but to start out for a clear objective. We may observe an illustration of the sinister result of wealth, as it has been asserted by the philosophers. On Saturday morning he had walked the streets with a feeling of careless security, almost of possession; now he traversed the same pavements with anxiety and apprehension. There was a similar thought in his own mind, but he put it differently. Before, he had wandered upon the streets as a hawk quarters the sky, lean and predatory and alert. Now he was like a prey-laden wolf, looking neither to right nor left, but seeking only the sheltered lair where he might batten at leisure on that which his teeth have seized. We may object that this metaphor is imperfect, as most metaphors are, but it gave John Rodney a very comfortable feeling as he crossed New Oxford Street, resolutely disregarding the unconscious constable who was directing the traffic at the point from which he had pursued the flying thief to St. George's Church, only forty-eight hours ago.

CHAPTER IX.

JOHN RODNEY, seated with his back to the wall, at the same table which he had occupied five days earlier, considered his position again. Senses of affluence and hunger had united to urge the ordering of a good meal, and it was not till he had consumed a liberal plate of steak-and-kidney pie, and was progressing more sedately through a double portion of suet roll that he felt in the mood to survey the field of action, and decide upon the tactics which it required.

He admitted freely in his own mind that the guns of the *Betsy Jane* had not yet thundered round with any remarkable consequence. But that did not show that he had not handled the privateer with a captain's skill. The knowledge which the morning had brought might be of a negative character, but it was no less essential to have it. He had the wit to see that such sums as his pockets held are not stolen or dropped about in the London streets without some outcry from their owners—unless those owners are at war with their fellow-men too openly to claim their help, or allow their knowledge.

Had he, he wondered, actually become possessed of a fortune which would be left in his hands without protest? Could he even cash the larger banknotes without any difficulty being raised? Might he not be doing an actual service to humanity by withholding the money from the particularly hardened criminal who might use it for very sinister purposes—perhaps, even, to hire assassins who would leave other shot-riddled bodies beside American or English pumps. Was he not doing this potentially noble action at the greatest personal risk to himself, knowing how certainly his own body, if his action should be discovered, would be objectionably plugged with lead in a similar manner.

Warmed by the coffee with which his meal was concluded, he began to plan for the retention of the money, and its realization. Suppose he should go abroad? To America, for instance. He supposed that, having bought his passage by the use of the smaller notes, he would be able to negotiate the larger ones in greater safety in an alien land. He could represent them, one or more at a time, as a legacy being sent to him from England, or as presents from an indulgent parent, to assist in establishing him in a new land. And he could use that thousand-dollar bill without difficulty as soon as he had landed there.

It was an additional evidence of the Napoleonic mind that even such details as that were not over-looked.

He could see only one difficulty. He had no passport. He knew enough of the procedure to recognize that John Rodney might have to commit wholesale and very dangerous forgery to establish an identity more plausible than the simple truth that he had come into existence during the weekend.

Considering how probably this vexatious detail might obstruct his plans, he became conscious of the isolation from his fellows which he had so light heartedly chosen, and a sense of loneliness, if not apprehension, such as he had not felt previously, invaded his mind. And it was while he was under the influence of this depressing emotion that a low and pleasant voice asked him if he would mind passing the salt.

He withdrew his eyes from the contemplation of the gangway of the liner, so difficult to ascend without the ticket-of-leave which modern governments issue when they transfer their citizens, as it were, from one jail to another, to observe the young lady whom he vaguely remembered as having shared the table with him six days ago. This was not one of the coincidences which are so frequent in the real drama of life, and so carefully eliminated from its fictitious presentations. It was a most natural thing. Those who sit at the same table in the same tea-shop at the same hour of the day will soon observe the presence of others who do the same.

Yet John Rodney felt a faint surprise, even a faint resentment, as he looked round for a salt-pourer which was not there. Even had it been so, the table was not large. She could surely have reached for it without opening conversation with a male stranger in that shameless manner. He was in doubt as to whether he should answer her at all, when he was disconcerted to observe the merriment in her eyes. Was it a joke, or some cryptic phrase, the meaning of which he was too innocent, or too ignorant, to comprehend? Then his glance followed hers, and he observed that the article she required was in his own hand. Not that he had been using it for his coffee, nor that he had required it for the suet-pudding which he had recently finished. He had been playing with it in idle fingers while his mind was on the undiscovered mines and unploughed prairies which he would locate or tame when he had overcome the difficulties of the intervening Atlantic.

"Oh," he said, "I'm sorry. I wasn't noticing."

"Yes, I could see that. Thanks."

Having said that, she gave her attention to the egg-on-toast which was before her, leaving him with a vague feeling of dissatisfaction. Had she shown a disposition to continue the conversation, he would have withdrawn into a diffident silence. Had she shown any evidence of shyness or self-consciousness, it would have silenced him as effectually. But she did neither, going on with her own meal very composedly, and taking no further notice of him. He had an uneasy doubt that she might think him a fool. And the feeling of isolation, of which he had been conscious when he was so disconcertingly interrupted to pass the salt, resumed its ascendancy. He looked at that alluring, indifferent face without remembering the wisdom of Villon, or that poet's own warning that it was of no practical value. When the waitress deposited a cup of tea at the right elbow of the consumer of the egg-on-toast, he stretched out an instant hand to pass a basin of sugar which was already somewhat nearer to her than himself.

"Thanks. I don't take sugar."

He was sure now that he was an object of amusement only. He remembered last week's absurd incident of the wrong check. Yet he felt that the impression could be removed if he could establish a more intimate contact. The Rodney spirit stirred at the thought.

"Do you always come here about this time?" He heard the words as though they were spoken by another, and was conscious as he did so of the appalling nature of such a question when addressed to a young and attractive stranger.

Dark-browed eyes, of a blueness not previously experienced by a waiting world, were directed upon him in cool but not unfriendly scrutiny.

"No. Do you?"

A voice that was low and musical curtness of the seven-lettered reply. There was some encouragement also in its interrogative, which invited the conversation to continue. With an increase of masculine confidence, Rodney avoided a direct answer—what would be the use of committing himself to a daily visit till he knew more of her own movements?—"I thought I saw you here last week."

"It depends upon when I can get away from the office."

There was no question in that. She seemed to have forgotten his existence again. But she was not going yet. She was giving the waitress a further order. She appeared to have as good an appetite as himself. He had finished half an hour ago, but there is no law against occupying a chair after a meal is eaten. The conversation had to continue.

"I come in any time. I've got nothing particular to do just now."

Fleda Collingwood considered him with professional interest. This was another, there was no doubt of that. She knew the signs. Did he need crushing? Scarcely that. She did not think him to be of an aggressive kind. Rather, it was a case for investigation. Who knew but it might even be— She did not recognize either his nautical or predacious characters. Her thought was that he might be rather a dear, but not fit to be out alone in a world where man-eaters abound. With feminine ease she took the opening that his answer gave.

"I suppose it isn't easy to get anything now while business is so bad, if you're once out. What's your line?"

It was a simple question, and one which he had himself invited when he opened such a conversation, but it was obviously disconcerting. He felt a disinclination to introduce himself as a master criminal, which did not originate solely in the reticence of discretion. Besides, he had done little yet to justify such a boast. Were he to say, "I decided to be a criminal, but have had some difficulty in finding out how to begin," he had a well-grounded doubt as to the way in which the information would be received. Even in poetic metaphor, were he to say, "I am a lean hawk hovering over the London streets," or "I am a prey-laden wolf, creeping back to my secret lair," it might have no better result. She might laugh.

He reminded himself in vain that the greatest criminals of history have experienced the fidelity of admiring women. All the evidence of literature may be gathered to support that position. Sir Walter Scott came appositely to his mind:

> "Lady, a nameless life I lead,
> A nameless death I'll die.
> The fiend whose lantern lights the mead
> Were better mate than I."
>
> Yet sung she, "Brignall Banks are fair,
> And Greta's woods are green.
> I'd rather rove with Edmund there

Than reign our English queen."

But perhaps if he had said that he was bent on living a nameless life, but wasn't sure how best to begin, the effect might have been different.

No, she might be repelled, or—very much worse—she might be amused. It was too great a risk.

She observed his confusion, and added: "I'm sorry if I've asked anything I shouldn't. You needn't tell me if it's the Secret Service or anything criminal.

She had no intention of making a good guess, nor suspicion that she might have done so. She expected that it was Art. She recalled the agonies which she had observed in a rather pimply young poet, when he had been struggling to tell her of the secret epic which had already developed to the extent of an unfinished prelude of seventy thousand lines. And he had written her six pages the next day, without a single allusion to her own eyes (which were really rather exceptional), all about how greatly he should value her opinion as to whether *silver* or *argent* might be the better adjective to describe the moon. To which she had replied on a postcard, *"Don't lose any sleep over that. Call it a Dutch cheese."* And that had been the end of him. Was she hooking another here? If so, he was not going to lay bare the secrets of his soul in a Lyons' tea-shop.

He was saying: "I only came up to London about three weeks ago. I've been thinking of going abroad, but haven't settled anything yet. I don't suppose I shall." He had realized while he spoke that it hadn't been a good plan. A man shouldn't set off rashly like that. Anyway, he should marry first. Women are notoriously scarce in the new lands. But this isn't a very good place to talk about things like that."

She looked at him with inscrutably friendly eyes, considering this remark in a doubtful mind. Was it a hint? If so, he was certainly coming on. She did not deny that he was a rather attractive boy. Was she going to fall in love with him in earnest? Not till she knew more, anyway. But she meant to find out. She was annoyed that her experienced heart was beating more quickly than usual, and she had a little difficulty with her breath (but nobody could have guessed that) as she said: "Do you really mean you've got nothing to do?"

"No. I've done what I came out for today. Would you—"

He hesitated for a second how to put it, where he should ask her to go. Obviously not to the sharing of Miss Sporethought's hospitalities. But she closed the pause quickly: "I've finished at the office today. I thought of going to Kew. You might come along, if you've got nothing better to do." She added, inconsequently, "There's not much fun going alone. I promised Johnny Williams he could come, but he's got measles."

John Rodney, amid the bewildering bliss of this unexpected development, felt a stir of jealous anger against the unknown Johnny. What right had he to a name which had been used by himself, if only for a few days? More important, what right could he ever have had to go to Kew in such company? But his jealousy declined as he considered the probable character of this absent rival. Had he continued the name, he felt sure that no one would have called him Johnny. Most certainly, he would not have developed measles at such a time. A futile, spineless man. How fortunate that he had not continued a name which would have been shared with such a character.

They rose together, and he stretched out a hand for her check in a movement which she frustrated easily.

"You tried that last week," she said, smiling. "But I'd rather pay my own debts."

They were both slightly intrigued as to what the other might think or mean concerning that remark, both knowing that she was deliberately misinterpreting the former incident, and they had an inarticulate feeling that they were getting on rather easily.

"It wouldn't have mattered. I've got lots," he said.

A remark which stirred a natural curiosity in its hearer. What was he really, and who? He was neatly but not affluently dressed. His tie hadn't cost more than three and sixpence, if that. Probably just careless about dress, as some boys are. Mary Daffern always said it was a good sign. Didn't think too much of themselves, and wouldn't want to spend it all on the wrong back.

"We'd better know who we are," she said. "My name's Fleda Collingwood."

"Mine's—John Rodney."

She noticed the instant's pause, and had a passing doubt. Was he reluctant that she should learn his name, or was it a lie? Was he the kind of cad who would not give his true name to a girl? Well, she would soon decide about that.

"It seems to be a case of Admirals All," she said lightly.

"Yes. Do you like Newbolt?"

"Yes. Of course. It's this way for the bus to Kew."

CHAPTER X.

IT was after ten, and the summer dusk was falling, as John Rodney, after twice turning up the wrong road, and once passing the house, owing to the disordered state of his mental processes, rang the bell (for he had not been entrusted with a latch-key) at Miss Sporethought's door.

It is always pleasant to wander in Kew Gardens on a sunny afternoon, when the chestnuts are flowering. Fleda must have noticed their attractions of sight and scent, for she had mentioned them at least twice, but to John Rodney (if that were still his name, which is difficult to say, as he was undecided himself) for all he had noticed they might have been spruce-firs, or even asparagus.

At 3:30 he had learnt that Miss Collingwood was a rather important clerk in the legal offices of Bletchworth, Inkfield, & Morrison. That she was an only child. That her mother was dead. That her father, she thought, was in Canada; but, wherever he was supposed to be, she always heard of him from somewhere else. That he sometimes sent her considerable sums of money when he was in funds, and cabled her to send as much as she could back when he wasn't. That he supposed her to be studying at the London University, but she had preferred to establish herself with a more regular and less flighty income than his remittances provided, generous though they often were. And that she shared a ground-floor flat, garden included, at 7, Hagen Road, Shepherd's Bush, with Mary Daffern, an arrangement of a nominally precarious duration because Mary was always engaged to be married to some one or other (usually other), but never did. Mary was an artist, employed by an eminent firm of antique dealers, and so skilled in her work that she had once been allowed to assist in the faking of an Old Master, which had actually deceived an expert at the National Gallery. Or, at least, she said so. Fleda said that you would like Mary, though (with an unusual lapse into Mary's own slang) she was rather a scream.

At four, he had returned these confidences with a very vague and mendacious account of the early life and experiences of John Rodney, the circumstances under which he had come to London, his financial resources and prospects, and the impulse which had induced him to consider the advantages of a wandering life.

At 4:30, when they were having tea together in apparent amity, he had absentmindedly pulled out a handkerchief in such a way as to scatter a quantity of banknotes to the winds of Kew.

As he had commenced chasing the notes, he had dropped the handkerchief, which Fleda had retrieved. She had appeared more interested than surprised when she had observed the initials which were marked upon it.

At five, she had been so kind to him with eyes and voice, and they had found so much on which they were in accord as they had talked of indifferent things, that he had been led to assume that they would meet again on a very early occasion.

At 5:05, she had let him know how much she enjoyed having an afternoon at Kew with some one who didn't give his own name. She enjoyed it once—but not more. At 5:30, by means of that definite hint, and without showing any eagerness for an amended narrative, she had Delilah-ed him into a somewhat expurgated but moderately veracious account of his thoughts and actions and experiences since he had arrived in London.

At six, she had led him to fill in the gaps and revise the inaccuracies of this imprudent confidence. And, after that, they had really talked.

Somewhat to his relief, and perhaps surprise also, she had not shown any visible emotion on learning that he stood, by his own choice, on the threshold of a career of crime. She had not appeared particularly impressed or even interested. With the practical sagacity of her sex, she had accepted the improbable truth as readily as she had rejected the more plausible imaginations which he had told her previously, and when she knew it she had held him down for two hours of talk, until they had parted at her own gate, to the single question, What was to be done with the money which had come into his possession?

If only Johnny Williams had not had the measles, he would have been the one to decide the problem. (Basil cursed the worm— under his breath, of course—what could you expect from a bally ass with a name like that?) He was sound in judgment, fertile in expedients, and with a knowledge of the branches of criminal law which the clients of Bletchworth, Inkfield & Morrison were specially addicted to violating, such as she did not profess to have.

But as the detention of the money being illegal in the absence of any means of identifying the owner—well, if she were Basil, she wouldn't be too sure about that. She knew the law to be a very intricate and dangerous thing, netting the feet of the unwary in sometimes unexpected ways. But it was also true that unsuspected rocks of refuge might be found by those with the skill to search, even amid the sea of penalties where the unguided guilty drown. There was no telling at all. But it was the sort of question on which Mr. Morrison's opinion would be particularly valuable.

The infatuated Basil had listened to the utterance of those alluring lips (they were really rather well modelled) with no disposition to dispute their counsel. It had been, indeed, a very great relief to find such a confidante, and to have his narrative received with such quick belief and in such a practical spirit. But was it the kind of tale to be lightly confided even to a firm for whom Miss Collingwood worked?

Yes. If Fleda were to be believed, it very certainly was. It appeared that Mr. Morrison would be very little interested in the moral questions at issue. They might interest Fleda, but not him. And even she couldn't help seeing that if the previous (we can scarcely say the original) owner were a desperate criminal (as seemed very likely indeed), it might be almost a public duty to deprive him of the means of doing further evil. That is, of course, if it could be done without flagrant illegality, or too much personal danger. Yes. It was a case in which Mr. Morrison's advice would be of particular value.

So they had parted at last, with the understanding that he would call tomorrow morning and see Mr. Morrison (and of course Ethelfleda), and he had come away with a feeling of relief that he had confided his problem to so intelligent and sympathetic a hearer, and enabled by that relief to concentrate his thoughts upon the thousand-times more important memories of the parting kindness in Miss Collingwood's eyes, and of a wilful strand of dark brown hair, and the arm softness of a chance-touched arm, and the things she had said or implied about himself, and other equally momentous matters.

Being, as we may have observed, of a direct and impetuous character, looking rather at the desired goal than the intervening obstacles, he debated in a pleasurably excited mind how soon he might put forward a formal proposal of marriage (if a formal proposal should be required for so obvious and inevitable a culmination) and had regretfully resolved not to risk the possibility that she might discover a lack of respect for herself if he should be too hasty in the assumption of her consent. He was, he knew, deeply versed in the subtleties of the female heart, and he saw additional reason for caution when he considered the ease with which she had detected the mendacities of his earlier narrative, and the prompt decision with which she had declined to continue their acquaintance on that basis. No, he would spoil nothing by lack of patience or self-control. He would wait years, if need be, for the certainty of so great a stake. Or, say, till Saturday.

Filled with such thoughts, even the romantic dreams of a successful career as a master criminal, which had occupied him for the past six days, grew dim in out-line and pale in colour. With the decision to place the problem of the finding of the pocketbook in the capable hands of Messrs. Bletchworth & Co., he felt subconsciously that he had rejoined his kind, and it was with a mind at peace with an ecstatic world that he rang Miss Sporethought's bell, and faced that lady in the narrow hall.

"Perhaps," she said, in a voice which she intended to be grim, but which might more accurately be described as agitated, "you'll tell me, Mr. Thornford, what it all means."

Waked abruptly thus from his dreams, whether of a girl's hair or a life of crime, to the challenge of his discarded name and the evidence of an insurgent reality, Basil Thornford replied with a coolness and self-control which gave some ground for hoping that he might prove equal to a greater emergency.

"If you would be rather more explicit, Miss Sporethought," he suggested politely.

"Don't tell me!" the perturbed female responded, as he stood silent, repressing an inclination to reply that he had no wish to do so, with a sound instinct that such flippancy would be ill-received, she became more explicit in her own way.

"Don't tell me, as you don't know. You comes here hiding in more names than you can't count, with the manners of a young gent as ever was, and you goes off for the day, and then there's them round the door as a decent woman doesn't want to know, and it's 'Does John Williams live here?' and 'Oh, it's Rodney now, is it?' and 'You stand aside, ma'am, we'll have a look for it in his room, if you please'."

"You didn't let them go upstairs?"

"How could I have stopped them, being two of the biggest brutes that you'd ever see? They'd have gone up whether I'd liked or not if I hadn't said I'd seen you take it out when you went, and

46

they wouldn't find it there if they searched till they were blue in the face, and it was that, or Constable West happening along the other side of the road, and I says 'out of my hall now, or I yells fit to wake the dead, and we'll see what the law says to them as gives a decent woman such a fright inside her own door,' so they says there's no harm to me either meant or done, and they backs out a bit, and I wasn't half long slamming the door, either. And then, when I went out shopping, there was the two of them at the end of the road, and if one doesn't follow me into every shop where I goes, and then they join up again when I comes back, and there they are now for all I know, though I expect they've had a few words with you before now, if they are."

"Then don't you think it might be a good idea if we close the door?"

"I'm not that sure as I ought to let you come in."

"Oh, yes, you are, Miss Sporethought. You see, you've done that already. There, that's better. Now suppose we go somewhere where we can talk it over more comfortably. I don't know whether they're still there or not, because I missed my way and went up the wrong road, and came down from the other end, by the canal. Of course they wouldn't expect anyone to come home by that way, but it seems to have been rather lucky for me. I rather think this is my lucky day. Now, Miss Sporethought, you've been a real sport keeping those men out as you did, and, if you'll come upstairs, I'll tell you what all the fuss is about, and tomorrow I'll have the best lawyers in London at work, and when they get on their tracks there'll be no more trouble for you."

CHAPTER XI.

"I DON'T want nothing to do with the law," Miss Sporethought announced definitely, as soon as she was seated, rather statuesquely, upon a hard chair against the wall of the room which she had let to this pleasant-mannered young gentleman of the many names. She was a brave and soft-hearted woman, and she knew that she was going to be talked over whatever the evil deeds that could be laid at his door, or the troubles into which he had fallen. The excitements of the day had not dissuaded her from cooking him a very appetizing supper, which she had insisted upon carrying up before she would listen to the explanations which he was prepared to offer, and every woman who is rather proud of her own cooking will know how difficult it is to be as angry with a man as he most often deserves while he is eating, with an evident satisfaction, the meal which she has prepared.

The remark was therefore of the nature of an insurance against the consequences of an impending fall. When the time for her surrender came she wanted one thing to be clear in advance. She didn't want anything to do with the law.

She was, in fact, a blameless woman with a dark past. For five more or less happy months, twelve years ago, she had reasonably supposed herself to be legally married to a commercial traveller, who had undertaken the investment of her modest fortune; and she had then opened the door to a. detective officer who had broken the news that she was last on the list of four matrimonial consorts scattered over the southern counties of England, without counting the one whose bones had just been dug up from a cabbage-patch in a Biddlescombe garden. With a pathetic fidelity, she had stood by the wretched man on his short and certain way to the gallows, and had assigned whatever could be recovered of her own money to the legal gentleman who had undertaken the profitable futility of his defence. After that, she had changed her name to as nearly as she could recollect that of the maiden days of her maternal grandmother, and moved from Balham to her present residence, with an excusable desire to avoid spending the remainder of her life in narrating her experiences to insatiable neighbours, and their unnumbered friends. To have to give her real name in a public court. No, that must be understood in advance.

Tactfully avoiding allusion to the meaning of the double negative, Basil assured her that there would be no occasion for her to do so. He had used the short interval while she was bringing up the tray to decide how much of the truth it would be wise to tell, and to contrive the decent draping of that which he felt need not be exposed too nakedly. He concentrated therefore upon the episode of the pocketbook, and emphasized the facts that his own money had been stolen, and that he was seeking legal advice regarding that which had been thrust upon him. He then completed his confidence by unlocking the suitcase and showing the pocketbook and the banknotes for £5,000 to his astonished landlady.

"I don't know as I'd 'a' had the nerve if I'd 'a' knowed that," she admitted with a frightened frankness. "I hope as you won't go out again, Mr. Thornford, and leave them be'ind here."

"I'll promise not to, if you'll tell me how you got on to that name."

"Seeing as it's on all your clo's—"

"Oh, yes, of course. Doesn't that show that I didn't really mind whether you knew or not?"

"I wouldn't say but it does," she admitted doubtfully. Basil's readiness in retort did not prevent a rather dismal inward realization of his deficiencies in the arts of the expert criminal, and it had been rather for his own justification than her deception that he had advanced this argument. After all, it had all been more or less of a game. He hadn't really cared.

He got rid of the agitated lady with the completion of his meal and the necessity for removing the well-cleared plates. She went down with the comforting assurances that sausages-and-mash had always been his favourite dish, and that Bletchworth & Co. would know how to deal with her unsavoury callers without any necessity for her to establish contact with the machinery, of the law.

But, being left alone, Basil lost something of the easy confidence that had been assumed for the pacification of Miss Sporethought rather than as an expression of his own feeling. It was no welcome knowledge that he had been traced to his new lodging, nor that he was being so diligently sought by men of the character which her narrative indicated. It confirmed his suspicion of the lawless nature of the man from whom the money had been taken, and it showed that he was not of a disposition to endure the loss. If he could not appeal to the law, it followed that Basil had nothing to fear from that direction. His peril was that his opponent was not likely to be deterred by any legal scruples, nor to shrink from any personal violence which would recover his property. There was, of course, the simple expedient of handing it over, but it was not one which Basil felt it at all palatable to entertain. He had lost £20 of his own money and, if he were right as to the characters of those with whom he was dealing, he had no assurance that they would reward an honest return, even to that amount, nor had he any proof that they had any better title to it than his own.

There was in him also a fighting spirit which resented the method of the approach which would have invaded his room in his absence, and as he considered the matter he resolved to resist or outwit them, at any rate till he had heard what Messrs. Bletchworth & Co. would advise. Perhaps the feeling that it would be a rather ignominious anti-climax to the evening's narrative, if he should have to call there in the morning with the news that the money was no longer in his possession, was not the lightest weight in the scale of decision. He remembered also that a continuing reason for calling at those legal offices might be of the first importance in the pursuit on which he had resolved—might be even a vital necessity if it were to result in a capture by Saturday!—and the money assumed a greater value as he pursued that thought to its logical and delightful end. When you meet a girl of such exceptional quality he saw clearly that the right thing to do is to marry her as quickly as possible. Why lose time? You might die. Think of that. And the marrying of girls is an operation which money assists. It may not be a vital necessity. It wouldn't be, if you hadn't got any. But if you have— yes, it assists.

He saw that there is much to be said for the creed of Rob Roy, as set out by the exemplary Wordsworth. "The simple plan" was particularly applicable to the present circumstances. Let it be open war.

And foul fall he that blenches first.

That was the spirit in which to operate. And what, in the name of the safety of five thousand pounds, was the operation to be?

He saw the probability that if he should go to bed, and get up in the morning in the usual way, it would be to learn that callers were at the door, and he had sufficient imagination to anticipate a very difficult interview. Or they might meet him outside. He wasn't sure that he would like that, either.

There was a third possibility, of an equally cheerless kind. They might come in during the night. The thought led him to switch off the light, draw back a curtain, and push himself between blind and window, to examine the state of his defences. The window frame was old and rotten, and fitted badly. A knife thrust up from outside would easily push back the bolt. There was a lamp almost opposite on the further side of the road, and by its light he surveyed a bare and silent road. The short summer night was not really dark. There was no sign of gathering foes. No ladder against the sill.

But he felt that he could not sleep without some better assurance that he would not wake with a pistol against his head. There was a heavy china ornament on the mantelpiece. With the aid of a spare bootlace, he suspended it from the window-bolt, so that if the bolt were disturbed it would bang against the glass, or, if it were cut, it would fall. There would be noise enough then.

But suppose they were to invade the house from the back—which would be a quieter and more probable way? There was no lock to his door. There could be no better defence there than the chair-back under the knob. He looked round for weapons. He was extraordinarily ill-equipped in that way, whether for a battle with desperate criminals, or a career of personal crime. His eyes rested upon the water-jug of his rather primitively furnished room. Flung with precision at a head intruding either by door or window, it might have a very quieting effect. He put it beside the bed.

Feeling that he had completed his dispositions for immediate battle, his mind reverted to the morning difficulty. Reviewing the probable course of events, he had a new fear. He saw that he must have been traced to his first lodging by the address in his wallet. From there he supposed that the two suitcases must have made him sufficiently conspicuous to enable diligent inquiries, assisted by the stimulating influence of a liberal expenditure, to locate him here. But he felt sure that Mrs. Postler would not have been dumb respecting her unpaid bill. Suppose that the police were already upon his track? Suppose he were arrested now, with this money in his possession, he would be in a very awkward hole. The most sanguine imagination could hardly see him emerge triumphantly acquitted, and with the money still in his possession. No, he had better leave during the night. He must hide or wander till he could call at the offices of Bletchworth & Co., and take counsel with those experienced lawyers as to his future plans.

But even this resolution was not easily taken. If his enemies lurked without, would he not be walking into their hands? Would he not be at their mercy in the deserted streets? Absurdly burdened with his two suitcases, would he not be equally incapable of defence or flight?

There was another risk. Men who walk burdened in the midnight hours may be questioned by the police. Probably are. What plausible explanation could he give?

But all these dangers did not alter the fact that if the two visitors of yesterday were waiting on the doorstep tomorrow morning, he would be faced by a very difficult interview.

It was a full hour after midnight when his final decision was taken, and then he did not venture to go to bed lest he might oversleep. He dozed in the fireside chair, with the jug beside him.

At about four o'clock, he roused himself, and packed his suitcases. He laid thirty shillings on the table with a note beside them "I think I'd better go early, but I hope this is enough." Then he went down the creaking stairs with his boots in his hand. He only ventured to bring one suitcase at a time, feeling that it would be the quieter way. It would be so easy to make resounding bumps on those narrow stairs, but when he learnt how much noise even one of them could make in the night, he regretted that he had not descended with a single rush, leaving his awakened landlady to call after him if she would.

But it was done at last, and he had put on his boots, and loosed the chain, and shot back the two bolts, and turned the squeaking lock, and there had been no sign of life either from Miss Sporethought or the lady-lodger whom he had not seen, but of whom he was vaguely aware as occupying the second floor, and he was walking a very silent, echoing pavement in the pleasant coolness of the summer dawn.

There was no sign of his foes. Should he meet a policeman, he had resolved that he would be the first to speak. There had been an old time-table in his room from which he had looked up the time of an early morning train that left Euston for the North. That was what he was going to catch. Could the constable tell him where he could get a taxi at this early hour? Boldness would be the best way. Do we not know that

…desperate valour oft makes good

Where prudence might have failed?

Of course, if he should regard him as a probable burglar, or recognize him as the young man with the two suitcases who left his lodging-bill unpaid— But to anticipate trouble is a very foolish thing.

The policeman was advancing from the further end of the empty street. Should he ask him about the taxi? He was less sure than he had been when he first thought of the plan. He was coming up the other side of the street. There was no need to cross over. He would just walk on in an assured way. But the policeman was crossing the street at a slant which was obviously intended to intercept him. A rather tall man, with long legs. It would be no use to run, even if he dropped his burdens. What a fool he had been to bring the two! Even if he'd known t hat half his belongings would be lost for ever, to leave them would have been the better way. Heaven only knew what he was in for now. He wouldn't ask about the taxi. Not to begin. Let the constable speak first. Perhaps nothing would happen if he just walked by with a confident air.

The experienced eye of the constable was upon him. He observed a young man who was obviously leaving for his summer holidays. One of those early morning trips. Perhaps ten days at Margate. The suitcases looked rather heavy. Probably some of Mother's home-made jam.

"Good morning, sir," he said, in his most affable tone.

"Good morning, constable."

It showed what could be done by a good nerve—and, of course, the Napoleonic mind.

CHAPTER XII.

AT 9:57 A.M. Basil walked into the offices of Bletchworth &
Co., and requested an interview with Mr. Morrison. After his nerve-
shattering encounter with the lengthy constable, he had found himself entering upon a broader road, and observed a sign-board bearing
the engaging legend "All buses stop here." He had not expected that
any buses would appear at that hour, but he had an inspiration that
he would have a more innocent appearance if he were standing waiting beside his luggage under the sign and his wearied muscles offered a supporting argument. He had not been there many minutes
before he was fortunate in the approach of an empty taxi, returning
to London from some distant hiring. He had driven to Euston, deposited his suitcases in the cloakroom there, washed, fed, and perhaps slept a little, and reached his destination with a sense of having
defeated an army of lurking foes.

The outer office of Bletchworth & Co. was evidently intended
for use rather than ornament. Its dingy linoleum floor-covering was
worn into holes. Its counter and desks were grimy. The centre of one
of its cane-seated chairs was a tangled hollow. Even on this pleasant
midsummer morning, it had an air of depression which was unre-
lieved by a patch of sunlight on one of its dirty plastered walls. It
seemed to share the despondencies of the constant stream of criminals who, with a retinue of their friends and alibis, occupied the four
chairs and the painted bench provided for the use of clients while
waiting an opportunity to narrate their woes. But there was no lack
of cheerfulness in the brisk demeanour of the five junior clerks who
shared the desks on the further side of the counter, and carried on
their multitudinous duties in the intervals of answering callers, prin-
cipals and telephones, being despatched on sudden errands, and
keeping up an almost ceaseless undertone of chatter among themselves. To them, it was a lively, happy and exciting world.

From one of these young men, Basil now received a prompt if
somewhat off-hand reception.

"Mr. Morrison? Well, you'd better sit down. He's engaged now. Not the Chislehurst case, I suppose?"

Basil denied the ambiguous distinction of being concerned in the Chislehurst case, of which he remembered vaguely having read something in the last week's news—a little matter of the abduction of a young girl under rather shocking circumstance for which one man was under remand (bail refused) and a warrant was out for another. He took the only vacant space, at the end of the wooden bench, beside an ill-shaven individual who sat oblivious of his surroundings, going over in his mind for the fiftieth time the romance which it had taken three days to construct. At any moment he might be told that Mr. Ducklin would see him, and if he could make Mr. Ducklin believe it—well, he wouldn't feel quite so much afraid of the witness-box as he did now. For Mr. Ducklin was not an easy man to deceive.

Basil sat quietly for a few moments, vaguely conscious of the atmosphere around him, of the black stubble on his companion's face, and of the two apprehensive bookmakers beyond him who were discussing the dismal prospect that it might mean a hundred quid to walk out of the magistrates' court that morning. Vaguely he was aware of a couple on the further side of the room who were discussing, almost to the point of a low-voiced quarrel, something to which the woman was urging, as it seemed, the reluctance of the man beside her. "You'd find," his voice rose for a moment, "if we had the sense to stand out—" They didn't look to be of any criminal sort. Normally, timidly respectable people. What evil had brought them here?

He might have been more acutely conscious of these surroundings, perhaps even more critical of the near aspect of these and other examples, nondescript and unsavoury, of the class among whom he had aspired to graduate, but that every sense was alert for sign of the presence of the one whom he had really come to see. Was it likely that she would be in a part of the offices to which he would not penetrate? Would he be shown into Mr. Morrison's room, and expected to leave after the interview, without seeing her at all? Surely, as she had known that he would be calling at this time, she might have contrived to have come out to speak to him? Had she not promised that she would introduce his troubles to her principal's notice? And now Mr. Morrison was "engaged," and he was not of sufficient importance even to have his name sent in, and of Fleda there was no sign. And it was ten minutes past ten now, by the loud-ticking varnished clock that hung high on the opposite wall.

Well, he would see this Mr. Morrison, though how much he should say was an uncertain thing, and then he would wait till she came out at lunch. It was a proof of the measure of his infatuation, which, had she known it, should have been for Miss Collingwood a very pleasant subject of contemplation, that she could so occupy his thoughts even to the exclusion of those who were on his track, and from whom he had fled through the night.

A clerk came in from the corridor. "Where's Miss Collingwood?" he asked hurriedly. "Mr. Ducklin wants her to take down."

"She's in with Mr. Morrison about something. You'd better tell Miss Tonks."

"He won't say thank you for that." The two youths grinned at each other.

Basil was inspired to action. He advanced to the counter. "I think Mr. Morrison might like to know that I'm here—while Miss Collingwood's with him."

The clerk to whom he spoke looked a moment's surprise, and a moment's doubt, and then gave a careless "Righto!" and crossed over to the telephone. "Gentleman here, sir, says you want to see him while Miss Collingwood's with you. Yes, sir, that's the name." He turned to Basil. "You can go in. Second along the passage on the left. You'll see the name on the door."

Feeling like one who, after an unpleasant interview with the Recording Angel, is given sudden unexpected access to Heaven, Basil crossed the corridor, and entered Mr. Morrison's room.

CHAPTER XIII.

MISS COLLINGWOOD, sitting at the further side of Mr. Morrison's desk, with a pencil in one hand and a notebook in the other, gave no sign of recognition beyond a quick lift of the eyes and the mere hint of a smile, but their effect was to draw Basil's attention so completely that his first attempt to establish contact with Mr. Morrison's hand went wrong by about two feet.

"I beg your pardon," he said, with nervous politeness. "I couldn't see very well at first. It was coming in from the light outside."

Mr. Morrison looked at him in his usual contemplative manner. Was he a fool? Was it nerves? Was he one of those partially blind people who aim to conceal their infirmity? He reserved judgment in a singularly acute and impartial mind.

"Miss Collingwood's been telling me of your adventure, Mr. Thornford. We needn't go over it all again, but there are a few points I want to clear up, and then we'll decide what's to be done. First, you'd better give me the Gower Street address—write it on this."

He pushed a memorandum-pad across the table and picked up his telephone. "Send Wilkes in. Well, then, get him."

They sat silent for the next two minutes till Wilkes appeared. Mr. Morrison sat looking at nothing, as though half-asleep. He was a man of rather gross and shapeless form, with a large, bald head, faintly fringed with light-yellow hair. His face was fleshy. His eyes small and pale. His hands were fat, and the thick fingers showed nails which had been cut or bitten back till the flesh bulged over them.

He never went into court, having no gift of eloquence, or such graces as are supposed to influence the verdicts of juries. His power was exercised in that room, which he never left during business hours, and such hours were long in those offices. He gave his opinions definitely, his decisions without hesitation. He was never hurried. And he was seldom wrong.

In defence of the criminal population to which the majority of Bletchworth & Co.'s clients belonged, he had a singularly unprejudiced—his enemies would have said unscrupulous—mind. But he had his own code. There were things which he would not do, nor permit. And he would have absolute obedience. If a client questioned his methods or declined his advice, there would be no resulting argument. He would be politely but instantly told that it would be better for him to go elsewhere.

"Wilkes," he said, as that alert youth entered the room, "take a taxi at once to this address. Tell the lady that you've come from Mr. John Williams to pay his bill, which he was unable to do when he left last week, as she was out at the time. Tell her that he would have sent before, but he's"—he paused a moment, and then added deliberately—"had the measles."

There was a look of excusably puzzled surprise on the clerk's face, for he had a colleague of this not uncommon name who was away from the office with that malady, and he knew that it could not possibly have been he who had been staying at Gower Street, but he had learnt to do what he was told without needless questioning. He only said: "How much ought it to be, sir?"

"You won't question that. She won't know that you don't know. You'll pay what she asks."

"We can't have any fuss about that," he explained, turning back to Basil as the clerk left the room. "When that's done, you'll be clear of the law, unless she's got a warrant out before now, and we'll know that in an hour's time. Can you describe the man who took your wallet?"

Basil did his best. "Not very clear. Had he a little scar over his left eye?"

Basil could not say more.

"I understood you saw his face before he picked our pocket. Red tie?"

Yes, Basil remembered that, though he wouldn't have recalled it without the suggestion. He had seen it distinctly.

"So I supposed." He turned to Miss Collingwood. "Tell Peters to let Rafferty's gang know that I want Bolshie Joe here at five tonight. Tell them it's important—for him." He addressed Basil again. "None of the money gone?"

"No. I've got it just as it was. I've been spending from what's left of my own."

"Good. I'd better look at it."

Basil brought out the notes, and passed them over. Mr. Morrison looked at the neat little packet of £5,000, and tossed it, with scarcely a glance, into an empty wicker letter-basket which lay on the desk beside him. He examined the smaller notes with greater care, giving a close scrutiny to such marks or writing as appeared upon them, but he made no remark, tossing them one by one into the basket. When he came to the £100 note with the five £1 notes, and the attached memorandum, he gave them a thoughtful pause of consideration, and spoke for the first time: "I'm afraid you're up against something here. Same pound notes, I suppose?"

"Yes."

Mr. Morrison touched a bell on his desk He passed the basket of notes to the clerk who entered "Have these listed fully. Numbers, marks, dates, everything. Keep them together as they are. Have it done at once, and bring them back."

Basil watched the departure of the wealth which was not exactly his, with an anxiety which was only partly allayed by the last three words. But for his confidence in Miss Collingwood, itself lacking in well-seasoned foundations, he might have made some audible protest against the way in which the money had appeared to be passing from his physical possession. As it was, he tried not to be anxious. But Mr. Morrison's next words gave him something else of which to think.

"I can't tell you yet whose money you've picked up, though I've made a rather likely guess. We'll go over the other papers you've got, and when we've done that I hope I shall be able to tell you more than I can now, though Miss Collingwood tells me they haven't meant much to you. But, if I'm right, there's only one of two things to be done with that money, and one's to hand it back to the man it came from just as quick as you can, and make your mind up that your own's gone; and the other is to put it in the strongest safe you can find, and lie low while we argue it out. And before I can tell you which I advise, I want to be a good deal surer than I am now whether he's on your track already, or whether you really gave them all the slip when you bolted from Gower Street. If you'll tell me just—"

"There's no use going over that. I didn't give them the slip." Basil proceeded to relate the reception which had met him on his return, and his flight during the early morning hours.

Mr. Morrison looked almost disturbed. "You should have told me this as soon as you came in. Did you mention our name to the woman last night?"

"Yes. I think I did. I wanted to reassure her." Mr. Morrison's hand went to the telephone. "That you, Peters? Get through to Prothero's Hampstead office at once. Tell them that there have been two men hanging round the end of Rushton Road, watching a house there, Number—what is it?—Number 74. I want to know by phone whether they're still there, and, if so, who they're from. Tell him to ring me up from the nearest call-office. I'm waiting to know. And now, Mr. Thornford, let's see the pocketbook, and the rest of the papers."

There was silence during the next few minutes, as the lawyer examined the documents, one by one, without comment, punctuated only by the return of the basket of money which had been so carelessly handed over to the outer clerks.

As the silent moments passed, Basil forgot the ostensible object of his visit in contemplation of eyes which declined to meet his own, for Ethelfleda Collingwood was quite clear on one point. She was not going to flirt—even if she had felt in the mood, which she was not quite sure that she did—before the eyes of Mr. Morrison, who saw everything, even when he didn't look.

Mr. Thornford was a client whom she had introduced. That was doubtless why she had not been dismissed when he entered the room. If the time should come when the firm would have completed his business in such a way that it would be receipting a substantial bill, there would be a five-pound note for her, or it might even be ten. That was the way of the firm. But she was not going to represent the young man in any other capacity, after telling Mr. Morrison that she had never set eyes on him till yesterday. She kept her pencil ready, and her eyes on her idle notebook.

Mr. Morrison spoke at last, in his slow, deliberate way: "If I am right, from these indications, of which I have little doubt, as to the ownership of this pocketbook, I must advise you, Mr. Thornford, for your own safety and peace of mind, to give us instructions to return it with its contents on such terms as we can arrange, whether bad or good. You would, I am bound to advise you, be in grave personal danger if you should delay to do so."

"Do you mean legal danger?"

"No, I don't think you need fear that at all."

"Do you mind saying whose you suppose it to be?"

"Not when I am sure. That is a point which I expect to clear up during the day. I cannot mention names till I know."

"May I ask if you think it belongs to any client of yours?"

"No. If I am right, he is not a man for whom we should act under any circumstances."

"What sort of man is he?"

"He is a blackmailer of international notoriety. Our general view is that all men are entitled to such defence or protection as the law provides, even for those who would have been outlawed, and so placed beyond its pale, by an earlier code. But we have always drawn the line at the defence of blackmail."

Mr. Morrison looked at his watch, as one who calculated, then he went on talking, as though it were his object to pass the time.

"There are two people calling here this morning who will have a very pleasant and unexpected surprise. Last month they dismissed a chauffeur without notice, or he walked out. Accounts differ. He came to us to sue them for board-wages in lieu of notice, and we issued process accordingly. On preparing the case for hearing, we found his tale to be uncorroborated, but he was relying upon the evidence of two previous servants, who had left more or less in the same way. We found that he had known one of these men—had known of both incidents—before he applied for the position. He admitted to me that he had threatened his employers, when he left, that these former servants would bear witness against them. Talking over his evidence with him, I formed two opinions. One was that he had applied for the position with an intention of leaving in the way he did, the other was that he was depending upon their reluctance to come into court under such circumstances, rather than upon the strength of his case, if they have the resolution to do so. They are calling here this morning, probably prepared to settle the claim. They will be told that there will be no appearance for the plaintiff, and they have consequently nothing to fear. I am telling you this anecdote, Mr. Thornford, so that—"

The telephone rang, and Mr. Morrison picked up the receiver without haste, but without troubling to complete his sentence.

He listened without interruption to the message which he received, and then said only: "Tell Peters to have a taxi at the door in three minutes. I shall want him to go to the Porchester Vaults." Then he turned to Basil. "Mr. Thornford," he said, with a quiet seriousness, "I'm afraid there's no time to lose. They were, as I supposed, two of Buddy Callaghan's men. They had, it appears, knocked at No. 74 several times without obtaining any answer, after which they withdrew down the road. Then Miss—your landlady—came out, and they intercepted her, and asked where you were. She thought she would be doing you a good turn, and scaring them off, by telling them that you had come to consult us about them. Ten minutes ago, following this interview, they hailed a taxi, and directed the driver to the Pelican Hotel.

"I cannot tell what Callaghan will do when he knows that you have come here, but he is certain to have some of his gang outside within a few minutes, who will watch your movements, if they do nothing worse. It is fortunate that his men appear to have gone to take instructions from him, instead of coming here first. I have ordered a taxi, and will send a man I can trust with you, so that you can place this money at the Porchester Safe Deposit Vaults. After which, you had better make your way to some retreat that he will not easily find, and let us have your address. You'd better phone it, not write."

While he spoke, he drew a large envelope from a drawer at his side, into which he pushed the handful of notes, and passed them over.

But Basil did not offer to move. He did not like being bustled off in this way. He wanted to know more. He wanted to give his own decision about the money. Above all, he had thought of a better plan for communication than by telephone. An absolutely splendid plan. He said: "I suppose you mean that this man, Callaghan, is staying at the Pelican?"

"Yes. Half London knows that."

"Then we've got five or ten minutes, anyway."

"Yes. Unless he has anyone near here whom he can get on the phone. But it's foolish to lose time. I never run needless risks."

Mr. Morrison spoke without haste, but he evidently expected his client to go.

"I won't lose any time, but I want to say one thing first. I've been thinking about this money, and I don't want to hold it back simply because it belongs to a crook who daren't ask the police to help. But I want what's fair. I want my own money repaid, because I lost it through picking this up, and I want ten per cent as a finder's reward. That's only what the police make you pay if you lose anything on a bus. If he'll agree to that, you can tell him he can have the rest. I'll let you know where I am a safer way than writing or phoning. I'll call at Miss Collingwood's address, if she doesn't mind, and send a message by her. They'll never guess how I keep in touch with you, if I do that."

Mr. Morrison looked at Fleda, with a raising of interrogative brows.

"Yes, I don't mind," she said coolly, "if you think it's a good plan. He can't call here, unless he means to be followed back to wherever he is."

"Very well. That's understood. But, as to the ten per cent business, it's what the police do, as you say. As to whether it's good morality, or even good law, we've no time to discuss now. But that argument won't help you with Callaghan. He won't pay ten per cent if he thinks he can get it off you in a cheaper way, and perhaps not even then if you've made him feel a bit raw. There's only one safe place for you now, and that's where he won't look."

"Who is he?"

"He's an American gangster who's specialized in blackmailing the police. He used to boast that he was the safest man in Manhattan, because he'd written a diary and deposited it in a secret place from which it's to be published if he dies in any unorthodox way. But he must have got scared about something, because he came over here about three months ago."

"Why don't they send him back?"

"Because it's turned out that he was born in Liverpool, so he's an English subject; and there's nothing against him here. Yes, Peters, you were quite right to let me know. Mr. Thornford's coming at once."

CHAPTER XIV.

IT was certainly puzzling. Basil happened to know the location of the Porchester Safe Deposit. Not, perhaps, sufficiently well to have walked straight there from Mr. Morrison's office, but quite well enough to know that the way did not lie through Bloomsbury's less frequented streets. They must be at least a mile out of their way. He remembered that Peters had spoken to the driver in a very familiar manner as they had got in. Evidently it was not a taxi hailed at random from the street.

He looked at the clerk who sat silently beside him. A third young man, with a colourless, very lean face, from which the cheekbones rose prominently; he seemed regardless of Basil's presence, and yet curiously alert and watchful.

Was he being abducted to some quiet place where he might be robbed, and perhaps murdered, with impunity?

He recognized some improbabilities in this idea, and yet it *was* queer; and £5,000, which is in such a position that it is extremely difficult for anyone who loses hold of it to make legal claim for its return, is an unusually tempting bait. It was true that it had been out of his possession already, and had been handed back, but what more natural than to have done that to allay his suspicions, causing him to bring the money in his own pocket to the place where it could be safely and finally taken? It was rather a humorous method, as though he should be politely cajoled to carry the essential rope to his own gallows.

Well, if it were really so, was it better to challenge the position at once, while they were still in the crowded streets, or appear unsuspicious until there might come some opportunity of escape? Perhaps a sudden dash from the taxi when they stopped in a traffic block. But the door on his side might be secured. He remembered that Peters had made a point of his getting in first, so that he sat by the unopened door. He must try it in such a way that no suspicion would be aroused should the ruse fail. "I think I'll get out a moment

while we're standing here. There's a tobacconist just over the way."
What could be more natural than that? But they were not running
through crowded streets. They had just entered a very long one,
which was almost bare of vehicular traffic from end to end. It was
rather impatience to end a doubt which he did not seriously believe
than a well-founded judgment that caused him to say: "Going rather
out of our way, aren't we, Mr. Peters?"

"Rather," that young man answered, in very hearty agreement,
and with a smile which would have disarmed a more cynical ques-
tioner than Basil was ever likely to be, "we've come about two miles
the wrong way, but we turn here."

"May I ask why?"

"Well, we started the wrong way, in case we were being
watched; and we came here in case we were being followed. Not
that we could have got away any easier if we were, but I just wanted
to know. You see, you can never tell for sure in the crowded traffic.
But we've had some long straight runs, with a clear road in the rear,
and we've dome some quick turns in between. There's no one behind us now and, if they followed at all, they know that I'm taking
you back to your room at Hampstead, or some other lodging up that
way. If they see me get back, they'll know I've taken you a good
distance, by the time I shall have been away."

Basil had a pleasant feeling that he was in very capable hands,
but he would show his own caution and foresight also. He answered,
in a low voice, looking at the driver's broad back.

"Unless they make inquiries and find out."

Peters smiled again. "They won't get much out of Wylie. He
may give them a hint of where we put you down, somewhere in
Golders Green, if they press him too hard. When Linstead jumped
his bail—but that's telling." He became silent, and then added more
seriously, "But I hope we got away without being seen. We don't
want any trouble with that crush."

"You think they're dangerous?"

"Yes, and so will you before long, if you have the pluck to hold
on to that cash. You won't think, you'll know."

"Should you hold on to it, if you were I?"

"I don't know. I expect I might have a try. But it wouldn't show
that I'd got much sense, if I did."

"But you wouldn't think it wrong to keep it? You'd only hesitate because of the risk?"

"Wrong? Not I. It's either money he's just got hold of by
blackmailing some one in the States, or it's what he'd got ready to

bribe some one here to do some dirty work. Probably both. You'd be doing good if you cleared him out till he hadn't a dime left. But you'll let the guv'nor pay it back, if you value your own skin."

"I'm not going to hand it back, unless I'm obliged. Not without my ten per cent, anyway."

"You'll find he won't pay that. He'd reckon he'd have his pocket picked once a week, if he did. He's more likely to want to make you a dreadful example of what happens to those who don't leave him alone. He'd probably think it was better business if he did that, and lost the lot."

"But I didn't pick it."

"He wouldn't call that the point. If you hold him up for a ten per cent, there'll be plenty of others to think they can do the same. You see, when a man once gets the wrong side of the law, he's got to reckon everything out in a new way."

"You don't think it's worthwhile?"

"What? Going crooked? It's a mug's game at the best. They mostly end in the dirt, and if they make a pile it never does them much good. They can't do anything with it worthwhile."

Basil considered this verdict on the romantic career on which he had decided five days ago, and which had already lost some of its actuality amid the supervening excitements, in a silence which was broken again by his companion.

"I'm not advising you to hold on. It's the other way. But, if that's what you mean to do, I might give you one or two tips that wouldn't do any harm."

Basil expressed a suitable gratitude for this very friendly over from one who had such exceptional opportunities for studying the ways of the criminal population of London, and was so interested in the information he received that it seemed that it was but a moment before the taxi slowed down in Chancery Lane, and Peters said: "We shan't stop just at the door. We'll drop you here, and you can walk on. We'll watch that you go in safely, and then clear."

CHAPTER XV.

AT half-past three that afternoon, Basil Thornford sat in a Piccadilly restaurant, and considered his position, which had become a rather frequent occupation during recent meals.

He had transacted his business at the Porchester Safe Deposit, and devoted a further hour to some other matters which had been suggested by his conversation with Mr. Peters. With commendable heroism, he had resisted an almost overwhelming impulse to go to the tea-shop in New Oxford Street where he might have hoped to meet Miss Collingwood. He had still to find an abode for himself and to fetch his luggage from Euston, before he made his evening call upon her.

Surveying the events of the last twenty-four hours he was conscious that they merited a satisfaction which he did not feel. During that short period he had made the acquaintance of a young lady whom he had decided to marry before the week closed—if not earlier; he had been introduced to a firm of solicitors who appeared to be exceptionally suitable to his peculiar requirements; he had been successful twice over in eluding his pursuing foes, and, as a result of that skilful strategy, he had been able to deposit the money in a place of security. It did seem enough for one day. And now all that remained was to go into some quiet retreat, and await report of the progress of Mr. Morrison's negotiations with his unscrupulous adversary, which was to reach him by the most desirable channel. Indeed, when he added the events of the day, he had failed at first to give himself due credit for that last stroke of Napoleonic genius. And yet it was when he thought of tonight's interview that he had this uncomfortable feeling of dissatisfaction. He felt that he had allowed matters to pass too completely into the hands of Bletchworth & Co., however competent they might be—too completely, that is, for the heroic attitude which should be maintained before the girl whom you have decided to marry. Particularly if the enterprise is to be consummated by Saturday next.

It was an instinctive resentment at the complete direction that Mr. Morrison was assuming, not only of the money, but of his personal movements, in the divine presence, that had caused him to be rather slow and argumentative in leaving his chair when that gentleman, without consulting his views, had ordered the taxi to be ready in three minutes; and the same feeling underlay his announcement of the terms on which he was prepared to settle, which had preceded his departure. He was not going to appear before her as a child in Mr. Morrison's hands.

He had another cause for serious reflection in the survey of his finances which he had just taken. It might have been a wise thing to deposit the whole of Buddy Callaghan's money, without taking anything from it, so to speak, on account of charges, and it was no less at his disposition than it had been previously, but it was a division that emphasized the diminution of his own resources. The £43 6s. 7d. which he had counted last Tuesday was now represented by no more than £22 0s. 6d. That was including the profit he had made on the stamp album. And he owed Bletchworth & Co. for settling the Gower Street bill, and for the taxi—no doubt, he owed them more than that! He was afraid to think how much it might be, but he had a feeling that they were not a cheap firm. There was even something ominous about the way in which they had undertaken those expenditures for him, without asking him for anything on account, as though they w ere mere petty cash items, too insignificant for separate consideration. He did not expect to see the twenty pounds again. This was all he had left, £22 0s. 6d., unless he should succeed in holding on to at least some of those deposited banknotes. And he would be needing money. Needing a lot. Twenty-two pounds wouldn't last long. He wanted to buy some flowers today. Expensive flowers. Heaven only knew what he might want to buy tomorrow. He thought vaguely of ocean-tickets, passports, marriage-licences, rings.

But the first question was: where was he going to stay tonight? Should he go to some humble lodging-house, trying to save every possible penny for the great adventure, or should he settle in a more lordly manner at some hotel which would soon consume the money he now had, recognizing that he was playing for a great stake, which retail economies would never gain? That would be the better, bolder way. What was the appropriate stanza?

He either fears his fate too much—

Yes, that was the spirit. He would go to a hotel. *Why not the Pelican?* In an instant, he recognized it for an inspired thought. It was there that he must go. Boldly, in his own name. He would see this Callaghan, who was so extremely feared. It was the very last place in which he would look to find him. It would be so safe an audacity. The name of John Williams might have been taken for his, or John Rodney, or even that of Rogers might have come to his enemy's knowledge, but in his own he would be secure. He made this resolution without definite purpose. It was of the nature of a gesture rather than a plan. The heroic attitude. It was for the observation of Fleda. And of course it would inspire her to admiration of the cool Napoleonic manner in which he was dealing with this emergency; and, in turn, she would inspire him to the mood in which victory becomes routine.

> A moment, while the trumpets blow,
> He sees his brood about thy knee,
> The next, like fire, he meets the foe,
> And strikes him dead for thine and thee.

Tennyson did express the idea rather well. Not that he was exactly applicable. There was an absence of brood. Still, you see the idea.

Under the impetus of this resolution, he called for his check, bestowed the three pence which still remained in a lonely pocket as the entire fruits of crime upon an indifferent waitress, and took the Tube to Euston, where he collected his suitcases, and, regardless of expense in the exhilaration of the new adventure, drove luxuriously across London by taxi to the neighbourhood of Victoria Station, and the Pelican Hotel.

Booking there in his own name, he looked round boldly and vainly for any fellow-guest whose demeanour might be suggestive of his truculent foe, and set out in a confident spirit for a pleasant interview at 7 Hagen Road, Shepherd's Bush.

Of course he would retain the money, or, at any rate, sufficient for the high purpose before him. And of course he would marry Fleda. It would do her good.

CHAPTER XVI.

"YOU mustn't come as early as this another time," Fleda said, sitting opposite to him in the pleasant ground-floor front which she had furnished herself to her own taste, and which she shared with Mary Daffern during the day, under a somewhat complicated financial arrangement which does not concern us. "That is, unless you're asked to tea. Mary mayn't be home for an hour yet, and we both like a meal when we come in."

The words were said with a smile, which disarmed them of their inhospitable sound, and Basil, being very far from slow-witted, recognized this easy familiarity of address as indicating a satisfactory stage of advancing intimacy. He thought also of the week's work which he had undertaken. It was Tuesday night now. Even a more sanguine temperament than his, assuming such to be possible, would have recognized that there was no time to lose. The two thoughts combined to inspire him to remark: "That would be rather jolly. I mean having tea with you first."

Fleda sat with a little table before her, still bearing the remains of the rather dainty tea which had been brought in on her arrival. She had her elbow on the table, and her chin in her hand. She looked at him with amused, self-reliant eyes.

"I don't intend to ask you to come before Miss Daffern gets in."

Basil was unruffled by this repulse. He said: "I thought it might have been better than staying late. We shall have a lot to talk about tomorrow night."

"We've got something now."

"Yes, of course. That's why I thought we'd better get the most important thing settled first."

"I might let you come to tea on Saturday. Mary'd be home then."

"I thought—" he said, and then stopped. He had felt equal to any audacity since he had booked that room at the Pelican, but even he felt that he might be going too far now.

But Fleda's curiosity was aroused. "Yes?" she said. "What did you think?"

Well, after all, she had got to know! "I thought," he said, with outward boldness which conveyed something approximating to an inward panic, as the words were spoken, "we might have been married on Saturday."

Fleda certainly felt somewhat startled at this declaration. But it was not the first (quite unsuitable) proposal of marriage that she had received, though scarcely after this fashion. There was a directness, a suddenness about this method which required—what exactly did it require?—perhaps, thought. She continued to look at him with the same friendly amusement in her eyes.

"Who to?" she inquired, and then added, too quickly for his reply, "I suppose you can, if you want to. I couldn't. Johnny's got measles."

"I don't see that we need worry about that," he said, declining the bait, but inwardly cursing the name of this invisible rival.

And then he had the discretion to change the subject as quickly as possible. After all, he had made some progress. She had got the idea! He had an inexperienced impression that a girl expects to be kissed in the early stages of these negotiations, but that it is a mistake to attempt it too soon. Say Wednesday, for that? He said: "But I've got one or two things to tell you. I promised Mr. Morrison I'd let him know my address. I thought it might be a good idea if I put up at the Pelican."

"At the—you mean where Callaghan's staying? It sounds mad."

She was certainly more visibly disturbed by this announcement than by his previous suggestion. He recognized her reaction with a well-founded satisfaction. He saw that the Napoleonic method triumphed again. He observed that Basil Thornford, acting as his own Intelligence Department, was a much more heroic figure than John Williams bolting fraudulently from his lodgings (but what could be expected of anyone with a name like that?) or even John Rodney fleeing through the summer night with a suitcase in either hand. He had a sound, instinctive perception of the fact that the male should crow, if he cannot sing. He should impress the female's mind, in the unavoidable interludes (or preludes) when he is not embracing her body.

But his satisfaction was somewhat modified by a change of expression on Fleda's face. She did not look impressed in the simple, desirable way that a female should. She looked anxious, even annoyed.

"We don't know each other well, but I thought you had more sense."

That was an annoying remark. Whether he replied, "Well, so I had," or "Well, you see I hadn't," it would be about equally satisfactory. People ought not to be allowed to make remarks like that. Especially not those whom you like so much that they are going to be married on Saturday—and what a time to wait! He said: "You ought to trust me about that."

"Trust you to have sense?" she asked, lifting amused brows. "I wonder why."

"Because I know a girl worth marrying when I see her."

There was inspiration in that reply. For a moment, it changed the subject. Fleda saw that there was to be no respite from these attacks, either from front or flank. She said, in the elliptical rather than illogical feminine way: "But I mightn't agree."

"Agree about what? If you don't think you're worth marrying, you're about the silliest chump—I mean you're quite wrong."

"I didn't mean that. I meant I mightn't want to marry you."

"Then who's being silly now? Of course girls don't. They have to be told. That's why they're not allowed to propose. They'd just go about asking the wrong men, and being sorry afterwards. Men that get measles, and things like that. When a man asks a girl to marry him, he isn't thinking of himself, he's thinking of her."

"You must be a singularly unselfish character."

"I didn't say that. I only said that I've got sense. I've been thinking about you all the time. I couldn't do anything much more sensible than that."

"You might do something a lot less. Like going to the Pelican Hotel."

"I don't see that at all. If they searched all London, it's about the last place where they'd look. He doesn't know me, and I shall see what sort of man he really is. I might sit next him at lunch. He might not be such a bad sort after all. I once knew a boy who was born in Liverpool, and he wasn't half bad. Suppose he were to confide in me about his loss. He might say he'd give a thousand pounds to have that pocketbook back, even for the memoranda alone. We couldn't make much sense out of them, but they may mean a lot to him. Sermons in stones and good in everything. You know you only see what you look for in this world. We weren't looking for anything good. And I should say, 'Put it on paper first, and the thing's done,' and we needn't go to America. We could go to Fiji."

"I don't think you need a wife. You need a mother. "

"Well, you can be both, and it'll save fares. But talking about that boy who was born in Liverpool made me think of something you ought to know. It's about his sister—a dreadful tale. And it's quite true. She's one of the prettiest girls you ever saw, or at least she was when she was young. At least, that's what he says. And she could have married some one when she was eighteen, but she wouldn't because he'd only got two thousand a year, and she'd heard of some one else who'd got three. And six months after, she was asked by some one else, who'd got a bit less, and by then she'd have been content with the two, but she didn't want to go below what she might have had. And since then some one's asked her every six months, and she always wishes she'd taken the one before, because each one of them's had a bit less than the last. And now she's twenty-seven, and those who ask her now have got nothing but debts, and her mother says, if she doesn't want to take the veil, she'd better take what else she can get, and no more nonsense about it. I shouldn't wonder if she'd marry a man like Johnny Williams, if he had measles all the time. It wouldn't really matter, after she'd got it as well. I'd better write to Bill, and get her address. She's somewhere at Tunbridge Wells, so it wouldn't be too far for him to go. Even if he went on working at Bletchworth's, he could go home at weekends. I'd write and tell him, only it might come better from you. I wouldn't mind doing him a good turn, if only he'll stop hanging round and pretending he's coming in first. The booby prize is more in his line, and he'd get it that way. It's no use looking as though you think I'm not serious. There's a lot of sense in it, if you think it out. And there's a warning in that tale that you can't miss. It's enough to make any girl wonder what she's going to get for supper."

"Wonder what—? Oh, I see. You're so picturesque. Yes, perhaps it is." Fleda laughed as she answered, appearing quite undismayed by the dreadful example of the lady at Tunbridge Wells. "But I'll say this for you, Basil. The more you seem to wander about, the more you come to the point all the time."

"You mean about marrying you?"

"I mean about anything. But I wish you'd listen to me for a few moments, and you'd know that this Callaghan business isn't exactly a lark. Mr. Morrison had Bolshie Joe in the office just before I came away."

"Did he make him cough up my twenty quid?"

"No, he didn't. Callaghan's got that. If you'll keep quiet for two minutes, I'll tell you what happened. I'm sorry for that boy. He's been scared to death from two sides. Callaghan says to Rafferty, 'Find out who picked my pocket, and send him to me.' Rafferty isn't one of Callaghan's men. He began by being a fence, and now he's the head of half the pickpockets in London. But he wasn't fool enough to quarrel with Callaghan. He just said, 'Right, Chief,' or something of that sort, and along Bolshie Joe had to go. You can see from that how Callaghan's looked at in his own world. They say he can shoot quicker and straighter than any man in the Bronx, wherever that is."

"It's probably just a tale," Basil interrupted. "I expect it means that no one ever saw him shoot anything. It's just what he told his gang to say about him, and they've repeated it till they believe it themselves. I expect, if he's got a pistol at all, the trigger's too rusty to pull."

"Well, I hope you won't be the first to find out. Anyway, Bolshie Joe went. At first he wouldn't say anything except that, when he found what he'd got hold of, he got frightened, and threw it away in the street. And then he says they tried putting a lighted taper between his toes—this was in Callaghan's own suite in the Pelican— and at first he couldn't tell, even then, because they'd gagged his mouth, so that he shouldn't make too much noise, and they forgot he couldn't talk while he was like that—"

"It just shows what a muddle-headed set they must be," Basil interrupted again.

"Perhaps it does. But it's not the kind of muddle anyone wants to get into, if they can keep out. When they remembered about the gag, Joe told them the truth, and they made him hand over your £20, as a lesson to him to be more careful next time, but he's to have half of it back, if they get all the money from you. So they got your address from him, and set to work to follow you. Rafferty told Joe he'd have to come to see Mr. Morrison, but he didn't want to know anything about what was said. He didn't want anything to do with it either way. I think even Rafferty's a bit scared. So Joe had to tell us— I was in with Mr. Morrison taking it down—and you could see him shake while he did it. 'You won't give me away, guv'nor?' he asked as he went out. Mr. Morrison said, 'No one's given away from this office. You ought to know that. But we may give Mr. Callaghan enough to think about to make him forget you. And don't you give away *that*'."

"Don't you think he will?"

"I don't know. But Mr. Morrison does. He may have said it on purpose. But I've been telling you the last thing first. Before Joe came in, we'd had Callaghan on the telephone, and Mr. Morrison talked it over with him. Callaghan said if you gave him his money back, you could have yours. He said he couldn't say fairer than that."

"Oh, couldn't he? What about the ten per cent plan?"

"He didn't seem to think much of that. At least, he said he'd see you fry in hell first. I believe those were his actual words."

"He seems to know where he'll be looking on. What did Mr. Morrison say to that?"

"He said he'd take his client's instructions, and communicate further."

"What does he want me to do?"

"He says it's the safest thing to give the money back at once; but, if you don't overvalue your own skin, you'd better lie low somewhere, and wait a few days while he's seeing what he can do. He says, if you don't mind the risk, he may give Callaghan something else to think of by about the end of the week, and it might even turn out that the money isn't Callaghan's at all, though it wouldn't follow that you could keep the lot. He says, if so, you'd better go somewhere where there are plenty of people about, and don't go out, especially not if you have messages asking you to. He said, just as I was coming out, 'Tell him to wait till the end of the week. I might have some news for him by Saturday'."

"By Saturday? I dare say he would, but I want it to be all over by then. That's the day that—"

"That's the day that you come to tea."

"That's the day we sail for—wherever the ship goes on that day. That's the way to decide. Leave it to chance. I don't suppose you really care so much where it is. It's a woman's whole existence making a man happy. Byron noticed that. But we needn't talk about it, if you don't want to. It's only Tuesday night now. Take no thought for the morrow's all right for you, unless you want some new clothes. I'll do the thinking about the rest. But what's Morrison really doing? That's what I wanted to ask, and when I look at you it puts me off."

"Then you'd better look at the clock. Good gracious, I didn't know it was that! Mary's long overdue now. Mr. Morrison's got something up his sleeve, but he wouldn't say anything about it to me. He scribbled copies of two or three of those memoranda out of the case. I dare say you noticed that. And he's been sitting looking at them most of the day. And just as I was leaving, after we'd had

Bolshie Joe, he got through to Scotland Yard, and asked for Inspector Cleveland."

"About Callaghan?"

"He didn't say, but I'm almost sure. Nobody hears when he phones. The exchange board's made so that they can't, and he made me go out just as the call came through. That's Mary at the door now."

CHAPTER XVII.

MY DEAR FLEDA,

I don't want to say anything against a man that's got measles, but there must have been a time before that, and if he wanted to, why didn't he then? He must have known you were old enough, so why didn't he when he could? Unless, of course, he's a child. But there's no need to be rude to him. People are always sent away after measles, and Williams is a Welsh name. Why shouldn't he go there? Tell him hillmen desire the hills.

Anyway, he doesn't matter. I don't see how he can be about again till it's too late to change, and I don't suppose you'd want to either. Williams isn't a really nice name. When you've had Thornford for a week or two, you'll see that.

But I expect you do now. But I don't want to waste time writing about him. I hope you didn't mind that I didn't kiss you before I left. The blood that blues the inside arm almost made me do it when you reached for Miss Daffern's cup, but my guardian knew a lot about girls, and I've heard him say that if you want them to make the pace, you shouldn't rush them too much at the start. So I'm going slow with you, and if it's a mistake I know you've got the sense to say so.

Besides, it wasn't only that. When I got up to go, I thought one or two couldn't have done any real harm, and then I thought that Miss Daffern might not have understood, and if she thought she ought to be kissed as well, and she seemed rather that sort, I didn't want to be rude.

But I had another thought on the way back, and I'm not sure that going slow hasn't been a mistake, so I thought I'd better write and explain.

It's about the passport having "and wife," which means that mine wouldn't do as it is, and yours wouldn't do at all, and I believe they take about three days to get, though I dare say if Mr. Morrison's clients are leaving England he may know of a quicker way. But it doesn't do to leave things till the last minute, and I thought you might like to go to America or else to Paris if you can speak French well enough, which I can't. And I don't believe in changing plans. It always brings bad luck if you do that. I expect you've noticed. And if we make a mess of our lives I don't mean it to be my fault, though I know I didn't do what I ought when I found you were alone when I got in, and I thought all the way back, suppose I got killed on the way back or tomorrow morning and never could, it would be just what I deserve, and "be sure your sin will find you out," and things like that, so I'm not likely to be so silly ever again. So, if I'm not waiting in the hall tomorrow night when you get home, I don't want you to be anxious about nothing, but you'll know I'm dead.

I saw Callaghan in the smoking-room about half an hour ago, as soon as I got back. I had a walk round, to see what I could spot, and felt sure it was he. He's the kind who thinks he's a gentleman, but it's a mistake. But you'd know him anywhere when you'd seen him once. He's a short man, not fat but very thick. The same thickness all the way down. And he had a big black cigar in the corner of his mouth, sticking up, like the pictures of Captain Kettle. I suppose that's part of the pose. But the queerest thing is his face. He's got a rather high forehead, and it's quite flat. The hair's cropped very short, and it grows along the top like grass on the edge of a cliff. And his eyes are quite black, and good-humoured in a cruel way. He'd got three toughs with him in what they thought were gentlemen's clothes, and they all seemed ready to jump when he looked round.

I sat down at the further side of the room, and ordered a lemonade, and when I'd been there a few minutes he looked at me, and then one of the toughs strolled over to my table, and said, "Anyone got this chair?" and of course I said "No," and he sat down, and asked me to have a drink with him, and I said I didn't want anything more tonight. And then he said in a whisper, as though we were talking in church. "Do you know who that is over there?" And I said, "No." And he said, "That's Buddy Callaghan," in a tone as though he'd said it was a man-eating tiger who hadn't fed for a month.

And I wasn't going to let on that I knew, so I said, "I've only been in London a short time. I don't know anyone yet. Is he on the legitimate stage, or does he just clown?"

He didn't seem to know how to take that at first, and then seemed to make up his mind not to get what he called "fresh." He didn't speak English, so I'm not trying to give you his words, but he said I was too ignorant to know how ignorant I was, and that Buddy Callaghan was the bummest racketeer in New York, and better known than the Prince of Wales.

So I took a better look at him, and said, "He does look rather that type. I wonder they let him come into a decent hotel. I suppose he messed things up there, and had to bolt? He looks rather a fool to me."

And then the fellow got mad, and said, "You'd better not let him hear you talking like that. He shoots quicker than he can think. If he heard you say that, you wouldn't have time to see it happen before you were no better than a piece of dead meat."

And I said, "Who's calling him a fool now?"

And I saw he didn't understand, so I went on to explain what a fool a man'd be who began that kind of game in a London hotel, and counted just how long he'd have to live, and I told him all about how they hang people in English jails, and tried to make it all as much alive as I could. And I asked him if he knew what it meant to be an accessory before or after the fact, and he didn't seem very well up in that, so I explained it as well as I could, and told him that I wasn't quite sure, but I believed they hanged them as well. I said they'd be almost sure to, if they were the kind of men who'd left their country for their country's good, and didn't really belong; and then I said, wouldn't he have a drink with me? But he thought not that time, and he got up to go, so I just said what pleasant chat it had been, and if he knew Callaghan, he'd better give him a word of warning to watch his step (I couldn't help showing him that I knew some American too), or the cops would soon lay him by the heels, and he'd wish he was back in Sing-Sing, or whatever he calls the hotel where he stays when he's at home But I shan't catch the last post if I go on.

Yours by Saturday,

BASIL

Fleda Collingwood considered this letter with obvious interest, while her morning bacon cooled. She said aloud: "Well, I suppose it's better than getting killed," but it was in a somewhat undecided voice, and she didn't say who it would be better for.

Mary Daffern looked up from her correspondence at the other side of the table, to ask: "What is?"

"Getting here a bit too soon." Mary Daffern spoke with the good-humoured tolerance of the expert for an amateur performance which she had happened to witness.

"You don't know how to manage your boys. I could marry that one in a month, if you'd hand him over to me."

"Yes, dear, of course. How long do you suppose I should take, if I really meant it?"

"Oh, I suppose you'd call it quick in a year, or perhaps two."

"You can try what you can do, if you like." Mary Daffern gave her friend a quick, questioning glance which she did not see, for she was reading the letter again. "Oh, my dear, I never poach!" she said lightly. "Besides, I've almost decided to marry Leonard Wilkinson. I shouldn't wonder if September sees the last of me here."

Fleda Collingwood looked up now with considering eyes. She seemed to hesitate on the verge of speech, while her resolution wavered to a decision. Then her lips curved to a smile.

"Race me?" she asked, with a confident challenge in her glance. "I'll bet you a new hat—"

"Done," said Mary, but she didn't feel quite so confident as she would have expected herself to do.

CHAPTER XVIII.

DEAR MR. THORNFORD,

You'll have to wait if you do.

Yours sincerely,

FLEDA COLLINGWOOD

(Can't you see that that's better than either?)

Fleda wrote that note at the breakfast table, before the cloth was removed, and felt rather pleased. She posted it on the way to the Tube, and reckoned that he would get it by the early afternoon post, and that it would make him think. So it did; but it had other consequences which must wait their place. She went on to her day's work, and it was nearly lunch-time before Mr. Morrison sent for her, he having been busy during the earlier morning with the Chislehurst case, and one or two other very interesting matters which it would be pleasant to turn aside to survey, but for the fear that we might never get back.

"I just wanted to know, Miss Collingwood, whether that young cockerel called last night as he promised, and if he's gone to earth in a safe place."

Fleda observed this mixture of metaphors without comment, as her position required, and said: "He's staying at the Pelican Hotel."

"You mean Callaghan? I knew that."

"I mean both."

She did not remember having seen Mr. Morrison so visibly startled.

"Do you mean," he asked, "that the young fool's trying to settle it over our heads?"

"No, I don't think so. He just thought he'd like a close-up of Callaghan, and it wouldn't be any real risk. I told him he ought to have more sense."

"No real risk? Does he think it's a play?"

"He says they don't know his real name, and wouldn't think he'd be likely to go there."

"What name has he booked in?"

"Basil Thornford, I believe."

"The young fool. Callaghan's had that name since yesterday. Yes, they got it from the woman at Rushton Road."

"Hadn't we better get through at once?"

"You'd better leave it to me, Miss Collingwood, if you don't mind."

Mr. Morrison gazed at his blotting-pad for some minutes. Then he rose heavily from his chair. "I think it's about time for lunch."

But Miss Collingwood unexpectedly stood in his way. "I think we ought to do something. He might get killed."

Mr. Morrison answered without showing the surprise that he may have felt: "Perhaps it might occur to you that it's his own look-out if he does. He shouldn't come here for advice, and then go off on his own line. But if you use the brains that you've certainly got, Miss Collingwood, it may enter your mind that the Pelican is a large hotel, and that Callaghan isn't likely to make a daily habit of reading down the names of the people who've checked in. There shouldn't be any hurry for a few hours. I don't suppose he'll be having drinks with Callaghan's lot. He's a bit too raw to get on that footing with them the first day. Anyway, I like to think first."

"But he did that last night, when he got back."

"Did what? Thought?"

"No. Got into conversation with them, or they did with him."

"How do you know that?"

"I had a letter from him this morning."

"Why didn't you say so before?"

"I didn't know that it mattered at first."

"I'd better see it."

"I don't.... It's not only about that. It's a private letter."

"You'd better let me see it, all the same. It will be quite private with me."

"You won't want to keep it?"

"No."

"It's a silly kind of letter, except about that."

"No doubt."

Mr. Morrison took the letter, and sank back into his chair. Fleda also sat down, knowing that his mental processes were less speedy than profound.

He read the letter slowly, twice over, from end to end, with an expressionless face, dwelling as long on the earlier portion as on that for which it had been given to him to see. He handed it back with the words: "You might do worse, Miss Collingwood. He's got guts."

Perhaps it was because she never did admire Mr. Morrison's metaphors that she made no answer to this. She took back the letter with a face as expressionless as his own. She asked as she had done before: "What are you going to do?"

"I'm not going to be in such a hurry that I do the wrong thing. Even if he does suspect something, it might give him the jumps. He's more than a bit puzzled, as it is. I'm going out to lunch now. You shall get Inspector Cleveland for me when we come in."

CHAPTER XIX.

THE Pelican Hotel is not one which can be recommended to single women of austere character, nor is it filled with Nonconformists at the time of the May meetings, but in spite, or perhaps because of, these deficiencies, its manager is particularly watchful not merely to suppress disorder among his somewhat promiscuous guests, but to avert occasions from which offences come.

He had not declined to receive Mr. Callaghan and his four companions when they had driven up to the door with three taxis of trunks, conspicuously labelled with the news that they had crossed the Atlantic in the first-class quarters of the *Île de France*, but after a rapid glance from his quick Italian eyes he had whispered to the reception clerk, who had offered them a costly suite along a corridor which was unoccupied at the moment, and had mentally added the value of the three rooms which they would not require in the price which he quoted for it. But Callaghan had not questioned the price. He was a gentleman. He always stayed at the best hotels, and would have been rather annoyed than otherwise at the production of a moderate tariff.

So he had that corridor to himself, until the hotel filled up as the season advanced, and the manager said, "If you're short of rooms, you must fill up 337 to 339, but don't put any women there." And when Basil walked up to the desk, and asked for a single room, without mentioning that he was going to be married on Saturday, the clerk said at once: "Yes, sir; we're rather full, but I can give you a very comfortable single room on the third floor."

Basil, surveying it at leisure when he entered that night, found it to be not merely comfortable accommodation, but luxurious after Mrs. Postler's and Miss Sporethought's accommodation, and the hospitality of his brother's attic, though it was actually smaller than any of them.

It was new to him to have a telephone at his bedside, and a reading-light that he could switch off after he had got into bed, and unlimited hot-and-cold, and a pleated paper cap to the water-bottle, and they all helped to give him a sense of assurance and impending victory. He felt that he was the captain of his soul, and his head unbowed without being bloody, which is far the more comfortable way. His little skirmish with Mr. Devlin (which was the name of Buddy Callaghan's satellite) had not diminished his confidence, and he felt some pleasure in the letter which he had just posted to his bride-to-be, his ever-more delight, though he couldn't help thinking of some of the things that he ought to have put in it but hadn't, as we all do.

Even the liquor-thickened voices of the Callaghan gang, as they came tumbling along the corridor soon after his own retirement, did not disturb his serenity. Indeed, he realized that they occupied the rooms opposite to his own with some confident satisfaction. What might he not overhear?

But the luxury of his bedroom did not induce sleep. He looked at his watch before getting into bed, and observed that it was after one. He didn't mind that in itself. He was too young to be upset by an occasional late night. It meant, at the worst, no more than a few yawns at the wrong times. But he had a shock of horror when he realized that it was Wednesday morning already. It didn't seem fair, when you had such a full week, that it should switch over suddenly like that. He felt that he was getting behind on points. If he let to-mo—today slip by, it would be Thursday, and, no, it simply wouldn't do. He hadn't made the pace as he should. Before he could go to sleep he must have to-mo—today mapped out in a different style. The night cometh, when no man can work. You can't help that, but you can use it to be Napoleonic in your plans for the coming day.

He remembered that it was one of the great warrior's favourite maxims that you should concentrate all your force on the main attack. Win that, and the rest will be yours at your own time. Was he making a mistake in extending his lines too far? Having a marriage to arrange as well as to take place within four days (which had all at once become three), was it not a mistake to attempt to clear up the Callaghan matter also within the same time? Having entrusted that negotiation to Mr. Morrison's very capable mind, would he not do better to put it out of his own? If it were not settled before he sailed (we may observe that he was inclined to confound this idea of going abroad with his main purpose, as though sailing were part of the marriage service), why should he not withdraw £500 as his commission, which he knew on the authority of Scotland Yard to be a quite proper thing to do, and leave the settlement of the rest till he came back?

Well, it would mean using one of the £500 notes, and there might be a difficulty about cashing it, even if he went boldly to the Bank of England, which certainly owed the money to some one. Suppose it had been stopped?

If the cashier said, "I'm afraid I shall have to ask you to step into the manager's room. This is a stolen note," he could reply, "Not at all. I am deducting my commission, as they do at the Lost Property Office." After that, the clerk might say, "That's all right, sir. I hadn't thought of that. How will you take it?" He might. But then again, he might not. Even Basil couldn't help feeling a doubt. He realized vaguely that the Metropolitan police are a law unto themselves as well as to the rest of the inhabitants of the London area.

Prudence counselled that he should content himself, for the moment, with the smaller notes. They would be sufficient for his immediate purposes. He saw that this decision was no sign of weakness. It was a further application of the maxim of his Corsican model. He must take no avoidable risk that might interfere with the main attack. Even coming to the Pelican might have been a mistake. But he wouldn't admit that. It had been a demonstration to impress Fleda. It was all part of the major military operation.

So, having eliminated the nonessential, he came to the real issue, and observed that Fleda—not unnaturally—might be the principal difficulty. Acting, as he had throughout, on the theory that a girl shouldn't be rushed, he had assumed too hastily that it would be sufficient to obtain her consent at any hour before Friday midnight, or on Saturday at the worst. He had once heard it said that a man could obtain a marriage licence without the consent or knowledge of the lady whom it was intended to honour, and had thought at the time that a prudent and affluent man would obtain a number of these documents, applicable to the desirable girls of his acquaintance, so that there should be no avoidable delay in case he should find the place and the time and the loved one all together, which he knew, on the authority of Robert Browning, doesn't happen any too frequently.

So there would be no difficulty about that. But he saw that the passport might be more serious. That should be dealt with at once. Couldn't it be done without prejudice? Being in a legal office, she would probably like the idea. Anyway, she would understand it at once. If he put it to her tonight, after she had been sufficiently kissed? But suppose she jibbed about that? He knew the uncertainty of a woman's moods to be proverbial in the mouths of men. Yet if he put it quietly and reasonably, that for all she knew she *might* feel she'd like to be married when Saturday came, and so, as a mere precaution, she'd better fill up the form? If you looked at it logically, the question wasn't whether she'd want to be married on Saturday, but *if* she were married on Saturday would she like to be unable to get away any further than Margate, when she might have gone to Switzerland or the Near East? Even a woman couldn't argue much about that. And, at the worst, well, she'd *have* to be rushed. After all, she seemed a sensible girl.

Having thus dealt with the questions of Callaghan, finance, the marriage-licence, and Fleda's passport, he was able to turn an easy mind to the consideration of the minor problems involved.

There was the question of where it should be. Not that he cared about that. Few men do. But he recognized that Fleda might. Well, he must remember to ask her. Even if she were awkward about everything else, she couldn't mind telling him that. Then he supposed he'd have to go and make the arrangements. It wasn't a thing he really cared about doing. Still, they'd be sure to be polite, or people wouldn't go there again. And, being summer, you wouldn't have to arrange for it to be warmed beforehand. Which showed how well he'd chosen the time.

Then he supposed there ought to be relatives, and flowers, and clothes, and, of course, rings. What a silly business it all was! The humouring of feminine fads. But the Napoleonic brain functioned again. It would be foolish to have any difficulties over little things like those. He would ask her what stones she liked best. He thought there would be a good deal to talk about to....

The dresses worried him most. He tried to persuade himself that they wouldn't matter much if they started off somewhere where they wouldn't be known as soon as the ceremony was over. And then Coventry Patmore did him one in the eye:

> "Now, while she's changing," said the Dean,
> "Her bridal for her travelling dress."

You only have to think that over two or three times to realize what a curse women are, even, or perhaps especially, when you're going to marry them next Saturday. And he saw that it would be risky to buy them himself, even if he measured her first, and to do that mightn't be as easy as you'd think. Not without her getting some idea of what he was at.

It was at this stage that his thoughts turned, not for the first time, to his brother's wife. He would go out as soon as he'd had breakfast tomorrow, and get some money from Chancery Lane, and whatever forms were necessary from the Passport Office, and go round to the shipping offices, and see where they could sail on Saturday, and then call on Ethel, and get her advice.

It was a very comforting thought. Ethel was never uncertain about anything. Ethel *knew*. It was like opening an encyclopaedia. And if she liked you—and Basil felt sure about that—she knew things in the right way. Not the way that makes difficulties. And with this pleasant resolution he went to sleep at last.

CHAPTER XX.

BUT when the morning came, Basil altered his mind about calling on Ethel. To begin with, he waked late—so late that Devlin, who was not an early riser, was crossing the passage to the dining room (for Callaghan's party had meals served in their own suite) as Basil came out of his, and was able to take the news in to Callaghan that the young gentleman who'd cheeked him in the smoking-room last night had booked a room close to them, and Callaghan, who had finished his own breakfast, chewed his cigar thoughtfully while he turned the idea over in a watchful, suspicious mind, for Buddy Callaghan was a worried man.

Then Basil had discovered that the charge for breakfast, an absolutely preposterous charge, was the same whether he took one course or five, and he felt that to content himself with his usual egg under such circumstances would be an almost criminal limitation. And, while he ate, he calculated the time that it would take to get to Chancery Lane, and then to the passport office, wherever that might be, and then to the office of the steamship companies, which he knew vaguely to be at the lower end of Regent Street, and he remembered that his brother sometimes got home to lunch. He didn't want to see *him*. And then he thought of changing the order of his programme, and remembered that Ethel often went out in the morning. He might get there at eleven, and have to wait for an hour, or even more. He had no margin of time for such errors. It would be best to write, and say that he would call tomorrow. Besides, he would know more by then, having seen Fleda, of the nature and extent of the assistance which he would require. And there would still be about two days. He had two well-founded impressions. One was that no woman was ever too busy in the history of the race to go out and buy clothes, whether for herself or others, and the second was that she could buy enough of them in two days to ruin a millionaire. So he went into the writing-room, and sent this letter.

PELICAN HOTEL, S.W.1,
June 17th, 1930

MY DEAR ETHEL,

Don't tell Devereux, because I don't want him
butting in, so I'm putting that first, in case he's about
when you open this, but I've had a busy time since
left him a week ago.

There's lots of money to be made in London, if
you look round, and take the chances that come, and I
think I've done that.

I'm getting married on Saturday, and going
abroad. I've got plenty for that, but I may come back
later and make some more.

I want you to give me a few hints on how to run
the show on Saturday, so I'll call tomorrow about
eleven A.M., and you needn't have any lunch for me,
unless you're sure that Devereux won't be home. It
wouldn't be any use to ask him to be best man, and if
it would I shouldn't know what it was for, but if you
like to come and be best woman, I should be rather
glad than not.

Yours with love,

BASIL

He read this letter over with a feeling of vivid satisfaction at the
astonishment which it would be likely to cause, and then carefully
obliterated the address of the Pelican Hotel, and substituted c/o
Bletchworth, Inkfield & Morrison. It made little difference, as the
only available envelopes had the Pelican crest embossed upon then,
with the address below, but at least it made it plain that he didn't
want any interference there, if Devereux should hear of what was
going on. Devereux had spasmodic attacks of conscience, and what
he would do during such visitations was beyond forecast, but it
would always be unpleasant for those on whose behalf it was agitated.

After that, he had quite a good morning. He collected some
money from the safe deposit, and renewed the affluent feeling which

comes, particularly w hen we are young, from a bulging note-wallet. He went to the Passport Office, and had a most courteous and sympathetic reception. It appeared that a passport could be issued complete in as little as two hours, including photographs, if the lady and he should attend together, each with an eligible witness. The difficulty regarding the subsequent change of the lady's name and status was not new to them, nor were they without an appropriate method of overcoming it. He went on to Lower Regent Street and was somewhat bewildered by the number of luxurious liners that were leaving on Saturday to various destinations in North and South America, Africa, Australia, the Mediterranean and the more distant East. He felt that it would have been easier to decide had there been a smaller choice. In a moment of comparative sanity, it occurred to him that it might be wise to leave the final choice to the bride-to-be, on which he made a collection of many gaudily printed pamphlets setting out the spectacular attractions of distant countries, and omitting their discomforts.

He hesitated upon an announcement of the cruise of a palatial liner which had been diverted from its usual routine to convey its patrons to the Land of the Midnight Sun. The midsummer advantages of Scandinavia must be clear to the meanest intelligence. It sailed on Thursday. It was now Wednesday, midday. No passports would be required. It could be managed quite easily. There might be a good deal to do first, but why not sit up to do it? An occasional late night doesn't hurt anyone. Besides, in a hot midsummer, isn't it better to be visiting healthy Northern fiords than catching fever in Algiers? And all at the cost of going to bed rather later than usual. But he put it down reluctantly. He knew that he regarded these questions with a cool and mathematical mind. It was no use wasting time over a proposal which she would turn down. There would be plenty to talk over without that. So he returned the pamphlet to its varnished rack. We can't blame him for that. We know what women are.

It is not surprising that he felt hungry at the end of these wanderings, and had some lunch in Piccadilly before he took a bus back to the Pelican. His pockets bulged with banknotes, passport forms, and travelling propaganda; his mind approached distraction with the number of things of which it tried to think at once. He saw that, if he were to allow no oversight, to commit no ghastly blunder, he must be systematic in these final stages of the Great Adventure. What he really needed was to make notes. But he had left his fountain pen in his room. It was a weakness with him, leaving that pen. While the bus jolted its way to Victoria, he must confine himself to the broad outlines of the programme. When he got back, he would make a complete list of every detail, and allot its sufficient hour. (He must have some new shoe-laces. He mustn't forget that.) And when he had worked everything out, and decided what Fleda must do herself, and how far Ethel must help and got it neatly listed, which might take all that was left of the afternoon, he would be able to concentrate a mind at ease upon the problems of conduct emotional tactics, and cold, convincing logic, which might arise at the evening's interview.

Disconcertingly, he remembered the most famous line in one of the most famous books in the literature of his native land, *First catch your hare*. But he put the warning aside with a steady will. Even Mrs. Beeton hadn't suggested that the hare couldn't be caught. Hares *are* being caught continually. So are girls. Think of all that have been caught before now. Millions. They are too many. You simply can't.

Still, suppose she did jib? What would the appropriate procedure be? Of prior importance, what should the procedure be to prevent jibbing? He saw that if the petty done the undone vast was not to become even more worrying than it was now, it was a case in which prevention would be far better than cure. He must consider this matter in earnest. Should he embrace her first, and leave the details to a later hour? Or should he say, "You needn't say yes or no, but just suppose we *were* going to be married on Saturday, just look at these books, and say whether you'd rather sail on the *Gigantic* to America, or on the *Southern Cross* to the Amazon?" Turning with a cunning, casual hand to the alluring views of the *Sports Deck* and a *First-Class Cabin*. Or, "Suppose I *did* buy you a ring—you needn't say you agree, but suppose I did—would you like diamonds alone, or a few pearls or rubies, and do you think platinum's really better than gold?" And then when she would be hypnotized and drowned in such seductive visions…. It was a difficult choice.

There were minor details of procedure, also, about which he would have been glad to have a more confident knowledge. Should he, for instance, begin by kissing her on the lips in the vulgar-looking Hollywood manner? Or would it be better to start on the brow, and work downwards? Should he proceed by sudden assault, or a deliberate approach which would make his intention clear? Faces gradually nearing like a slow-motion picture, at ten yards an hour. Hollywood again. He had a sound instinct warning him to avoid Hollywood. Fleda had a sense of humour. He had no intention of sharing the fate of the gentleman who had been recommended to the Dutch cheese.

Faced by these problems, and with the end of his journey approaching, his agile mind recalled St. Paul's resort in a similar difficulty. He recognized vaguely that he was confusing great matters and small—though it may be well not to inquire which he was disposed to place in either category, but the idea was applicable.

He would put such questions from his mind, and rely upon the inspiration of the event itself. From the moment when he got in he would concentrate upon the practical side of the enterprise, as a man should. The decision may have been sound enough, but he was destined to spend the afternoon in a different way.

CHAPTER XXI.

AS Basil entered the lobby of the Pelican Hotel, he observed Mr. Buddy Callaghan standing at the reception counter renewing his supply of cigars, but he would have passed him with little heed. Had he not decided to concentrate on the one vital matter? He had referred him to his solicitors. And Mr. Callaghan, his mind on other things, and his eyes on the cigars which he was inserting into his case, would not have seen him at all, had not the clerk, with something more than the usual attention to the correspondence of hotel guests, called out, as Basil passed, "Oh, Mr. Thornford, there's a letter for you." He had, in fact, received it from the postman, and put it into its appropriate niche, less than five minutes earlier, and, Basil being a new-comer, had had a moment's hesitation as to who he might be, which had fixed in his mind both the letter and the one for whom it was meant.

Basil was surprised. He was expecting no correspondence. Surely Ethel couldn't have answered by now? He approached without enthusiasm, half expecting to receive a communication which he could hand back, as not being for him. When he reached it, the letter was already laid on the counter, in full view of Mr. Callaghan, and the two members of his bodyguard who formed the smallest retinue with which he ever appeared in public.

As Basil picked it up, plainly addressed in a rather pretty, but very plainly formed feminine hand, *Basil Thornford, Esq.*, the black eyes of Buddy Callaghan were fixed upon it, and then lifted to himself in an angry, suspicious stare, which he might have observed at another time, but that his heart was beating with a sudden excitement. It was not Ethel's large, emphatic hand. It was a letter from Fleda. None but Fleda knew of his location here. Even his self-confidence—and we may have observed that diffidence was not his greatest fault—did not prevent an anxiety that made it difficult to delay opening the letter before the liftboy's eyes, and then hesitate to do so when he got to his own room. He must be cool, Napoleonic.

She must have had his letter of last night when she wrote this. What was there in its contents to have produced so prompt a reaction? Except, of course— He tried to recollect everything that his letter had contained in one instant comprehensive thought. And this envelope was so thin! Just a few words written probably on an angry impulse. Sarcasm, too, probably, like the Dutch cheese. He had a sudden clear realization that some of the things he said and did might wake derision in a hostile, even in a conventional mind. And women are inclined to be conventional. Suppose she didn't really like him at all?

Well, he wouldn't give up! Even if she told him never to call again. It was almost never, having to wait till tonight, anyway. You couldn't say there was much difference. He laid the letter down on the writing-table which was one of the features of that small, luxurious room, and resolved to have a wash before he opened it. He decided that if it didn't tell him not to come tonight it might say anything, and he wouldn't care. The unstable nature of woman has been known for centuries:

> Hear what Highland Nora said,
> "The Earlie's son I will not wed..."

And we know what happened to her.

Indeed, looked at properly, the worse it was the better it would be. And, anyway, not opening it till he had washed was a cowardly thing. Suppose it were to ask him to see her at lunch at the usual place? He didn't know how long it had been there. Or to meet her somewhere during the afternoon? Perhaps in ten minutes from now? And he wasting the time in this infernal funk!

It was certainly short. "You'll have to wait if you do." If that meant anything at all, it meant he could come early tonight. It meant that, *after* he had told her what to expect. And couldn't he see that Collingwood was better than either? No, of course not. Who would? It was a good name enough. Good enough for a start. But she must have had it for twenty years. Probably more. He had never thought about her age. She was just herself. He wouldn't have cared if she had told him she was quite old. Even twenty-five, though of course that would be absurd. Still, that wasn't the point. It had had a good run. By next Saturday it would be quite time for a change.

He was certainly in better spirits when he washed his hands than he would have been if he had left it unopened. He recognized the value of courage. Indeed, as he considered it further, good spirits became ecstatic in anticipation. It seemed to him at that moment, not entirely without reason, that the fight was won. He saw that she had begun to parley, and in a strife in which to parley is to give way. She had run up the white flag. Or was it red? He remembered Wendell Holmes's apposite lines:

> O'er girlhood's yielding barricade
> Floats the great Leveller's crimson fold.

We may observe a suggestion of Bolshevism in this pre-reference to its familiar flag, and its relation to Love may invite research. Perhaps extremes meet. But Basil was in no mood for such abstractions. He had become the conquering male. All the same, the flag was white rather than red. It was hard to imagine a very blushing surrender from Fleda Collingwood. There might be passion enough, half-awakened, behind those amused, considering eyes. But there would be coolness, poise, perhaps even a light, self-mocking humour, even at the greatest moments of life. Basil did not articulate such thoughts. He became intoxicated with the assurance of victory, with the desire for the physically adorable, the body which expressed her soul. But the consciousness was there, the realization of what she was, even as it expressed itself in the tone and terms of that cheerfully-derisive note, which he yet recognized for what it surely was. He had demanded the keys of the citadel, and she had answered with—a flag of truce. And he had only known her for a week! Really, rather more—or less—than that. Could you count from the first casual meeting? Well, perhaps you ought. And then it had been, "Good luck has he that deals with none." What a fool he was! But of course he was younger then. Since the second meeting, he could not reproach himself with many wasted hours. And there were men who wasted years of life in slow "engagements," or even without making any definite selection for this high adventure among the million of delightful English girls which surround them. What utter fools men are!

By this time he had put the towel back on its rack, and sat down at the writing-table, still in conquering mood, to tabulate the requirements of the next two days, which must clear the path to heaven.

He wrote rapidly, his mood making light of difficulties. When you faced it in the right spirit of enterprise, how easy it all became!

Rings (two).

Licence (consult Bletchworth's. Fleda undertake this?).

Place (get this tonight. Arrange tomorrow).

Where to go (settle this tonight. Thousand miles up Amazon too hot?).

Passports (Bletchworth's do witnessing? Go together?).

Own clothes (not exceed ten pounds. Remember laces).

Ethel 11:00 A.M. tomorrow.

1st *Note*—Must know time boat train leaves before fixing time ceremony (Friday, if necessary).

2nd *Note*—In case of....

"Put up your hands!"

It was the voice of Mr. Devlin of New York, and the face of Mr. Devlin confronted him as he looked round, showing the compressed lips and scowling expression suitable for such occasions. Basil saw also the muzzle of a rather large and sinister revolver levelled in his direction.

There is no certain way in which any of us, hero or coward, sage or fool, will react to the same circumstance. Health and mood will dictate the widest differences. Basil might have been more amenable to this suggestion had he just received a letter of a different tone. As it was, he recognized its absurdity in a buoyant mind. He said briefly, without moving his position: "Don't be a fool."

Mr. Devlin felt a natural anger. He had not been told to kill this objectionable young Britisher, but to fetch him to Mr. Callaghan's room. He had carried out his instructions in the most exemplary manner, crossing the softly-carpeted passage and opening the door noiselessly, and surprising his victim with his hands harmlessly employed at the writing-table. What more would you have? He had spoken the magic words in the right tone, and, as surely as the sun sets in the west over God's Own Country, the young fool should have raised his hands. He felt that he was confronted with a different technique, and was without instructions or experience for dealing with such an emergency.

Basil, on his part, after his first instinctive exclamation, was not entirely at ease. It did not occur to him to elevate his hands. He knew that he would look silly, which no Englishman is readily prepared to do, and his reason told him that his life was not in any imminent jeopardy. Still the position was unpleasant. He knew that his heart had hastened its pace, though less vehemently than when he had seen a letter on the hotel counter half an hour ago. He felt vaguely that he ought to say something soothing, preferably in the man's own language, but in the excitement of the moment, he could think of nothing except *Mind your step—hot baby—O.K., Chief,* and *sign on the dotted line,* none of which seemed appropriate for crude administration, though, in a more leisurely moment, two or three of them might have been worked in.

Mr. Devlin was the first to break these seconds of considering silence, which may have seemed longer than they were.

"Fool yourself," he replied; "you've gotta come to the Chief s room."

"Who's the Chief?"

"Mr. Callaghan. You'd better look smart, with less jaw."

Basil felt some increase of confidence with the knowledge that the question of the altitude of his hands had been quietly dropped. It was first blood to him. But he had had time to realize that he was in a really unpleasant position. He had some hundreds of pounds upon him, which, whatever their earlier origin, had actually come out of Mr. Callaghan's pocketbook, and which, for all he knew that gentleman could identify; and he had good reason for thinking that he was alone in this wing of the third floor with anything from three to five of the worst gangsters of New York, who may be inferior to the Chicago variety, but are sufficiently formidable. He might as well go to them, as that they should come crowding in here, and it would show that he wasn't afraid of anything they could do. Also, it might get him the interval which he required to rid himself of the money, which he didn't mean to lose if human ingenuity could retain it for the semi-sacred purposes to which it was destined. He said boldly: "I want to see Mr. Callaghan. Tell him I'll be over in about three minutes."

"I reckon you'll come along now."

"Then you reckon wrong. I've got as much to say to Mr. Callaghan as he has to say to me, and some things he ought to hear, but I'm not going to be bullied by you. I'm coming over in three minutes, and you're going to tell him first. It's no use trying to act here as though you were in New York, and got the cops squared."

"I guess you'll come now, or—"

"Then you've got another guess coming." That was good American, anyway. How easy a new language is! "You can tell him that if I'm not over in his room in three minutes, he can come here with all his gang, and start the fireworks too, if he's made up his mind to die in his native land."

"And find the door locked like as not?"

"Haven't I told you I mean to come? And couldn't you blow out the lock, and only get two years' hard? And isn't that better than getting hanged?"

Perhaps Devlin thought it was. He certainly thought that it would be better for the Chief to handle this racket himself. He saw, also, that if they once got this young rooster into their own room they might be able to make him crow in a different key. He said: "Well, I'll trust you for that, but if you try guying the Chief, you'll be sorry, or you'll be the first that's got away with it yet. You'd better not try bolting down the passage, either. There'll be two open doors on the way, and you'll sure learn how a bullet feels."

He looked round the room, and picked up the telephone which he broke deliberately, still keeping the pistol pointed at Basil in the conventional way.

Basil didn't like that. He had had a thought of using that instrument at the back of his mind. Besides, the ruthlessness of the destruction made more real the characters of the men in whose hands he had placed himself with such foolish rashness. But he hid his thoughts with some success, as he said: "I suppose Callaghan's going to pay for that." And then, in a final effrontery, he called after the sullenly withdrawing Devlin, "And, I say, if you *do* come back before I can get across, just remember to knock. You don't walk into people's rooms in this country without knocking. You've been here long enough to learn that."

The gangster made no reply. Basil, congratulating himself on the fact that the key had been in his pocket, lost no time in locking the door.

CHAPTER XXII.

"HE'S our client," Fleda said boldly, "and I think he ought to be warned."

"When you're a partner in this firm, Miss Collingwood—"

"When I may be going to marry anyone by Saturday—"

Mr. Morrison allowed himself an expression of surprise. Fleda felt rather surprised too. She had not meant to say that. It was just the desire for an effective retort, and the nonsense in yesterday's letter must have put it into her mind.

"I'm afraid I hadn't quite realized the celerity—"

"But you read his letter."

"But not your reply."

"You don't suppose he'd have written a letter like that if I hadn't let him?"

Mr. Morrison wisely abandoned the argument. He said: "I think he's quite able to take care of himself."

Fleda looked at him with amazed eyes. She had always considered Mr. Morrison to be a sensible man. "He's no more fit to take care of himself than a baby in arms."

"No? Well, I'm sorry, Miss Collingwood, but he'll have to do the best he can—till tomorrow, anyway."

"I suppose you've got something on with Inspector Cleveland that you think's more important, and you don't care what risk he runs."

"You mustn't think in this office, Miss Collingwood. Not unless you're told. Not even if you *are* leaving to get married on Saturday."

"I didn't say that I was." She really hadn't meant to say that, and had a moment of panic at the idea of losing her very comfortable and well-paid position with Bletchworth & Co. "But," she repeated, with a woman's persistence, "after all, he's our client, and I think he ought to be warned."

Mr. Morrison became thoughtful, and she had the sense to remain silent. He was not sure that she was wrong. He even had an inclination to tell her how the matter stood. He had found her to be an exceptionally trustworthy and level-headed girl, but if she were in love— No, it would be a foolish risk. He knew that the contents of that pocketbook supplied the evidence which Inspector Cleveland required, and that warrants were already issued for the arrest of Buddy Callaghan and his four companions. He knew that, in view of the sinister reputation of the five men, it was intended to arrest them during the night, when they could be surprised in sleep, and the danger of armed resistance would be reduced to its minimum. He knew that the manager of the Pelican Hotel was a party to these arrangements, and would facilitate the movements of the police when the time came. Meanwhile, he had been asked to allow nothing to happen which could disturb them in any way. Even misconduct, if it should occur, was to be overlooked as far as possible till the right moment arrived. No, she mustn't know anything about this; but, after all, the young fool might be best out of the way. He said: "You mustn't overlook the fact that if he'd taken our advice he wouldn't be there at all, and I don't suppose he's in any danger now. It's about fifty to one that they don't know who he is. You can ring him up from here if you like, and tell him to clear out. But you won't mention Inspector Cleveland, if you please, even to him. I'll tell you one thing, Miss Collingwood, which you may find rather interesting. If this matter goes as I mean it to do, there'll be that £5,000 just left lying about, and it'll belong to whosoever hands it happens to be in at the last. If you have the sense not to interfere you may find it where you'd best like it to be, but if you come butting in it may end up at Scotland Yard, and your young friend asked politely to prove his claim, and where will you be *then*? I'll tell you this. If it once gets out of his hands, it'll need more law than I know to get it back. But you can ring him up, if you like."

"Get me through," Miss Collingwood was already saying, "to the Pelican Hotel."

"Well?" Mr. Morrison inquired, as she put the receiver down a few minutes later.

"They say he isn't in. They've rung up to his room, and there's no reply, so they suppose he's out."

"Well, that's likely enough, and the best thing too. He's not likely to spend his time sitting there. Seeing him tonight. Then you can tell him. But it won't matter by then."

"Do you mind if I leave early this afternoon?"

"It's rather a sudden impulse, isn't it, Miss Collingwood?"

"Yes." She hesitated, and then looked at her employer with amused eyes. "I think it's the heat."

"Yes," he agreed. "It's the heat. Probably you'll be better in the morning. And perhaps you'll be able to tell me by then whether Miss Simpson's to take your place."

But Miss Collingwood had left the room, so that he was uncertain whether she had had the benefit of his last words. Thirty seconds later she was saying, "Pelican Hotel, please—and rather fast."

CHAPTER XXIII.

BASIL acted quickly. He didn't want those men coming back to the door, and perhaps pushing in when he opened it. He didn't intend to have any of them inside it again.

He wasn't as clear as he would have liked to be as to what he should say to Callaghan when the moment arrived, but he was quite clear as to what he had to do first, and the sooner he did it, and got out of the door, the less risk there would be.

He turned the banknotes and most of his own money out of his pockets, keeping a little, because it might look odd if he carried none at all—would, indeed, indicate what he had done—and hid it quickly, by crawling under the bed, and pushing it beneath the carpet, at the further corner. He also turned out the passport forms and shipping pamphlets from his pockets, though he contented himself with throwing them into an empty drawer of the dressing-table.

He would not have admitted to himself that he anticipated having to turn out his pockets, or that he would submit to being searched. He was going to talk some sense into this Callaghan's head. But he had felt that the money would not be exactly safe if he should carry it into the midst of those whose claim to it might be considerably better, and was certainly no worse, than his own; and, if he left that behind, the other papers might as well stay also. They might certainly indicate a purpose of abrupt departure which might not be understood in the right way.

Hurried as he was, he gave a moment to brushing his clothes, lest they should indicate too clearly the crawling feat from which he had just emerged. Then he deliberately left the door-key on the dressing-table, and went out into the passage, pulling the door shut after him. He knew the chambermaid had a master-key. Probably there was a duplicate in the office. He could get in again well enough, when necessary. But if there should be any effort to persuade him to return for that money, or to search his room to obtain it—well, it simply couldn't be done. The door locked when it was closed, and could not be opened from outside without the key, or an unlawful and probably noisy violence. If he had not been so careless in leaving it unlatched when he came in he would not have been surprised as he was. Still, he would doubtless have opened the door. It might have turned out worse than it did. But it was no use standing in the passage like this. If he stood long enough, he might get absolutely scared. What was required was merely coolness and common sense. Most inopportunely, he recalled the tale that Fleda had told him of the torturing of Bolshie Joe. But they had been dealing with one of their own kind. One who would never dare to protest. Would they—another most inopportune doubt—regard him as a fellow-criminal too? Whether that were so or not—and it did seem rather likely—he recognized that he would be almost as loath as themselves to appeal to the protection of the civil power. Even if there were no risk to the money, legal proceedings of any kind would be a fatal interference to the ecstatic plans which had filled his vision less than an hour ago. He didn't wish to spend Saturday morning giving evidence against the criminal who had smashed his telephone.

These thoughts took but the moment in which he stood hesitating outside his own door. Then he shook them off, and walked over to Mr. Callaghan's reception-room. Through the crowded incidents of his own short career as a master criminal, or whatever may be considered a more suitable description, he had never needed the Napoleonic mind as he would be needing it now.

He had no occasion to knock. The door, which stood partly open, widened to admit him. A lean, sallow-faced individual with a curiously-projecting tooth, pushed past him unceremoniously, putting his head out to call: "Come along, Jake."

Jake came up the passage, and Basil heard the door close as the two men re-entered together. Heard, not saw, for his eyes and mind were sufficiently occupied by the reception which Mr. Buddy Callaghan had prepared.

There was a round table in the centre of the room, large enough to seat half a dozen people, and covered by a crimson cloth. Buddy Callaghan sat at the further side, with Devlin at his right hand. He had a pistol lying on the cloth before him. On the nearer side of the table there was an empty chair.

"Sit there," Mr. Callaghan said curtly. It was a command rather than an invitation.

"Thank you," Basil replied cheerfully. "I'm afraid I didn't ask Mr. Devlin to sit down."

His eyes met those of the gangster in the first exchange of a duel which both approached with hesitation, and it was an exchange in which both were baffled. Basil had described Buddy Callaghan's eyes as good-humoured in a cruel way. It was an accurate description of their normal expression, but there was more cruelty and less good humour now. Cruelty is the child of fear. Basil had an accession of confidence from the instinctive perception that the man was afraid. But it did not follow that he was afraid of him. Rather, he was exultant in the capture that he had made. Exultant—and yet puzzled. He did not understand how Basil should have come to be here, or what part he had in the shadow which had fallen across his path in this cursed London. Mystery is the parent of fear, as cruelty is its child.

"What's the game?" he said curtly, showing large, white teeth that closed hard on the query. A coarse, thick, well-shaped hand closed on the pistol-butt also, as though to suggest that its use might follow an unsatisfactory answer.

"There's no game on my side. I came here to offer you a fair deal."

"You came here to see me?"

"Yes. I thought we ought to be able to settle matters together."

"Settle what?"

Basil hesitated a moment. The question seemed to indicate that Callaghan had more than the recovery of the money on his mind. Something of which he did not know. But Callaghan might think he did. Or he might be trying to find out. He remembered what Fleda had told him about Morrison ringing up Scotland Yard. He tried to fence till he should learn more.

"I'm not sure that I do now."

Callaghan stared. Anger distorted his face. "You're not sure—" he began. Then he controlled himself to ask, "And why not now?"

"Well, you're not over-polite." Callaghan stared at him again in a moment of ominous silence, and Basil added, "As my lawyers have got it in hand, it might be best to leave it to them. They're a very good firm."

Callaghan's right hand tightened on the pistol. He raised his left and brought it down on the table with a violence that shook the room. He poured out a torrent of oaths, containing little core of meaning, beyond the assertions that Basil was foolish, and insolent and young, and was about to learn wisdom in unexpected ways. He appeared to be in a paroxysm of anger, but it was hard to tell how much of it was uncontrolled emotion, or a business pose. Devlin sat impassive while it proceeded. He was used to the Chief's ways, on which the gang thrived.

But it proved to be the wrong way with Basil. He said, "It's no use going on like that. We shan't get anywhere."

As he said it, he saw a moment's flicker of enjoyment in Mr. Devlin's eyes. That gentleman was still inwardly sore from the reception which he had met when he had reported his failure to overawe his unarmed opponent. Now the Chief was getting a bit of it too.

Callaghan may have recognized that he was not making the desired impression. He did not reduce the menace of his attitude, but he became more explicit in threats as he continued.

"Shan't get anywhere, shan't we? You'll get somewhere you won't like, if you don't sing in a lower note. Now you listen to me. There's four of us here, and another at the end of the passage to see we don't get disturbed, and I want my money and my papers back—every one, mind you, *every one*—and you don't go out alive till I've got them here. So now what do you say?"

"I say I shan't agree to anything while you talk in that tone."

"See this pistol?"

"Yes. It's plain enough."

"See those nicks? That's the men it's killed. There's nine there, and ten's better than nine."

"Not in this country—I mean it didn't kill them here."

"You young fool! Do you suppose you can't shoot yourself in your own room? And we rush in just too late. There'll be five witnesses here."

"Then there'd be five men to be hanged. When they don't know who it is, in this country they hang the lot."

Basil felt far from comfortable as to the outcome of this interview, but he was confident enough that there was no reality in these threats of murder. Apart from the position in which they would put themselves, it would not help them to recover the property which they sought. He felt also that courage and a show of confidence gave whatever chance there might be of emerging from the duel successfully. He added, "I never had a pistol in my life. Every one knows that. And Mr. Morrison knows why I've come here."

Callaghan looked at him satirically. "Knows that, does he? Then he'll understand when he gets a note from you to send me what belongs here. I'll give you three minutes to write it in the right way, and if it's not finished by then— Heard how we had to argue with Bolshie Joe?"

"You daren't try that kind of thing with me."

"You'll soon know better than that."

"You daren't do it, because you wouldn't dare to keep me afterwards, or to let me go."

"You'll go just as soon as we've got what belongs here; and you'll go with a quiet mouth. It won't be a tale that you'll want to tell."

Basil was not sure he was wrong about that. Was not sure either that the force of the threat did not lie in the fact that, if it were sufficiently serious, it might succeed without more than a demonstration of possibilities. He felt that the position required thought. He said, with some adroitness, "We needn't argue that. I don't think you quite realize how matters stand. I must just think it over a little, and then I'll tell you what I'm prepared to do."

As he said it, he had a renewed conviction that Callaghan had a fear of which he did not know the occasion, and with which he associated him in a worried mind. His eyes showed it, for an instant, at the expression "how matters stand." But, if so, it was hidden the moment after. He pulled out a heavy gold watch, and laid it on the table before him.

"You'll have five minutes to think, and if you're wise you'll think in the right way."

Basil tried to think. It didn't seem an easy thing to do to order, while the watch ticked the seconds away audibly in the silent room. Not the brilliant thinking which the occasion so urgently required. His eye fell on the pistol beside Callaghan's hand. If he suddenly pulled the cloth towards him, and the pistol came with it....

Callaghan seemed to guess his thought. At any rate, he said: "You won't try any tricks here, not if you're a wise guy. Just look round to the door."

Basil looked, and observed that the two men who had come in after him were still standing by it. The door was open. One of them looked out towards the passage. The other—the one with the projecting tooth—had a pistol covering him. It was not a pleasant thing to observe, but an irrepressible characteristic of his imagination caused him to observe that Mr. Callaghan was also in line with the weapon.

"I suppose," he said cheerfully, "it would be a good thing for the wall." And then added in explanation, "I mean that you and Mr. Devlin would stop all the bullets that missed me."

"We don't miss in this racket."

"I wouldn't be too sure of that. I might duck suddenly, just as they were loosing off. I don't see how you could complain about that. Of course you might hit them too."

This persiflage did not appear to improve Mr. Callaghan's temper. He looked down on the watch, and observed curtly, "Two minutes left." But it had had the incidental effect of drawing the attention of both the men at the door, and it was a general surprise when a pleasant feminine voice inquired,

"May I come in?"

With a smile curving her lips, which was belied by the observant gravity of her eyes, Miss Fleda Collingwood stood at the door.

CHAPTER XXIV.

CALLAGHAN leapt up with an oath. "Dancer," he roared, "what the hell—" He seemed to be unable to find words to finish.

Dancer stood at the door. A man with a waist and curled and plastered hair, who had once been handsome in a feminine, and yet vulpine, way.

"Chief," he said, "I thought I'd better let her come in. There were some folk on the stairs."

Fleda had walked into the room. Basil got up, and in the confused uncertainty of the moment no one appeared to notice. For a long second their eyes met in an oblivion that could not last, but that established an intimacy of understanding that may have done more for Basil's impetuous plans than he could have gained by a whole evening of the eloquent and ingenious persuasions that had been plotting in his fertile brain.

He offered his chair to Fleda, moving it to one side of the table as he did so. The action brought Callaghan's eyes upon him.

"Who told you to move?" he asked angrily.

"In this country we always offer a lady a chair." He turned to Fleda with a gesture of explanation. "I moved it to one side, because these gentlemen like to shoot each other over the table, and you wouldn't want to be in the way." He added, without waiting for any comment upon this fantastic misconstruction of the conversation, that she had interrupted, "I suppose it's really me that you've come to see." And then to the astonished Callaghan, "Miss Collingwood is from Messrs. Bletchworth & Co. I expect, if you'll excuse me for a few minutes, I'd better see her alone."

It seemed for a few seconds as though the audacity of the attempt might succeed. Callaghan stood silent, scowling, in an obvious indecision. Devlin sat impassively, as he had done throughout. Callaghan had said that he would show him how to manage this sort of business, and he was there to learn. Basil saw the bewildered uncertainty in Dancer's eyes. He had not known what was going on, but from the quietness of the room he had supposed, as he watched the end of the corridor, that the Chief was getting his own way, as he always did. The two men who had been at the door were of the kind that do as they are told. Brave enough in a brutal way, but leaving the thinking to others. A good bodyguard in Broadway or the Bronx, but somewhat subdued by the London atmosphere, where men did not step quickly from their paths, or whisper admiringly behind their backs. Who, though they did not carry guns had a disconcerting confidence in their own security. Vaguely they recognized that a population which is accustomed to put its hands up without protest is essential to the well-being of the gangster world.

Had Callaghan failed to assert himself at that moment, it is unlikely that any of his attendant gunmen would have barred their way to freedom, but, as Fleda rose from the chair on which she was scarcely seated, and moved with Basil towards the door, he waked to a sudden realization of crisis.

"Shut that door," he shouted. "Don't let them move!"

The two found themselves confronted by three men who stood before a closed door, with a menace of lifted guns.

"Give me the key of that door," Callaghan said, walking over, and dropping it into a side-pocket. "Devlin, I want to talk to you. Come with me, all of you except Dancer. Dancer, watch these two young devils, and put a bullet into either of them if they give any trouble. It's the safest way, and I'll see you through if you do. There's a clear getaway from here, if it comes to that. But *don't let them go*, or I'll shoot you like a dog with my own hand."

There was a second door at the side of the room which opened into his own bedroom. He led his followers through it, leaving Basil and Fleda in the locked room with their single guard.

CHAPTER XXV.

THERE was an interval of silence after Callaghan withdrew. Basil was conscious of appearing in something less than heroic attitude, and was in a state of more anxiety for what his reckless adventure might mean to Fleda than he had felt when he was facing a single risk. Fleda had an exceptional though somewhat impersonal knowledge of the criminal methods of two hemispheres, and its result was to make her very far from comfortable. The quick decision with which she had come to warn Basil was not inconsistent with a very lively annoyance that he should have been such a fool as to be here at all, and she had now to add to that irritation a feeling that she had not shown much discretion in coming as she had. She had just walked into a trap—and yet not exactly that, for she saw that her coming had been to Callaghan an unwelcome thing. Still, she felt that she had been a fool, which made two, and her temper was not improved by that arithmetic.

Besides all this, there was the fact that Dancer stood between them and the door only two yards away, and would share whatever confidences they might exchange.

Still, it was no use sitting silent there. She was about to say something, without being very sure what, when Basil began. The fact that he must maintain the heroic attitude—or how could he dominate his capture sufficiently to ensure the punctuality of Saturday's ceremony?—set the note on which he opened the conversation, with one of his usual erratic imaginations.

"It's like contract bridge," he said, with the best smile he could manage; "You've got to exchange all the information you can, without giving away more than you can help to the other side. Though it can't matter much, one way or other, when they've got such a rotten hand. Is it important—what Mr. Morrison wants me to know?"

"There's no hurry about that."

"I suppose he'll be phoning in about twenty minutes to know what's up when you don't get back."

"No, he won't. I've got the afternoon off."

Basil considered the implications of this information in a sanguine mind. He placed an interpretation upon it which was not altogether wrong and which raised his spirits considerably, but how exasperating it made it that he should be sitting there, when they might have been— He'd got to find some way out. It was absurd.

Should he just get up, and say, "I've had enough of this nonsense. Put that silly thing down. We're going out." And just walk past him, or knock him down?

The worst of that programme was that while he had felt almost sure that Devlin wouldn't shoot, he had a feeling, almost approaching conviction, that Dancer would. And besides that there was the little difficulty of the key being in Callaghan's pocket. And while he considered this Fleda spoke again: "There seemed to be a little hitch in the negotiations as I arrived."

"Oh, I wouldn't go that far," Basil answered lightly. "Mr. Callaghan's rather in a mess, and it interferes with his natural suavity. I suppose you noticed the absence of that serene repose that marks the caste of Vere de Vere. He simply hasn't got that. I expect he had it in early youth, and lost it abroad. Now, Dancer here would discuss any subject without losing his self-control. Suppose, for instance, we ask him how long he thinks the manager will be satisfied to have his third floor corridor used as a one-way street? He might ask Mr. Callaghan to leave, and think how awkward it would be, with all the packing to get done after four o'clock. It is after four, Mr. Dancer, isn't it? It must be almost time for tea."

Dancer scowled, but said nothing. He had been told to watch, not to talk, and to shoot if they moved. He would gladly do that, but as long as they sat still he must let them say what they would. But he was disinclined to speech, partly because he did not understand the position, and was ill at ease. Like all the gang, he wished himself back in the safety of familiar streets. They might not seem exactly safe from the London viewpoint, but he knew what their dangers were. There were dangers from other gangsters at times. There were circumstances under which the police might be troublesome. Even in New York, there are things that you must not do, if you wish for continued freedom, and to die of senile decay. Yet such limitations were few, and quite easy to understand. But to talk of being told to check out, because a manager didn't approve—! Why, in Hoboken once he had seen a hotel boss shaking like a jelly because Callaghan had just looked at him with his silent stare. And the worst of it was that he wasn't sure but that it might be true. If the Chief would only go back! Women were the deuce! He knew that from many episodes of his own experience.

But they were talking again. He'd better listen. Callaghan might want to know what their talk had been. It wasn't exactly a subject on which he cared to dwell. Fleda, after a hesitation as to whether Basil were going wisely in poking fun at his captors, or irritating them with most unpleasant suggestions, which we may possibly share, had decided that they might as well have a duet if he wouldn't stop, and was now giving her double audience the benefit of a somewhat detailed knowledge of recent blackmailers and of the penalties that had been inflicted upon them; and how Freddy Jones had howled in the dock when the judge, under circumstances which she purposely left as vague as possible, had thought that fifteen strokes with the cat would assist him on the difficult path of return to a virtuous life.

"Of course," she added, "it isn't really fifteen strokes, it's nine times that many, because the cat's got nine lashes. That's how many? Yes, a hundred and eighty-five. I expect you're right. I never was much good at mental arithmetic. It's that many at least, if not more. They say, after the first six strokes, there's not a bit of skin left on a man's back, unless it's exceptionally long, and after that it's just like lashing a piece of raw meat. If they're not strong enough to have it all at once, they stop about halfway, and nurse them back, and give them the rest a few months later. The last time they gave it to a man in Pentonville, they say he screamed so that a prisoner went mad in the next cell."

Fleda chatted without giving any attention to Mr. Dancer. She was just narrating some of her office experiences to her companion to pass the time. Talking shop, as we are always too ready to do. But Basil watched his face, and saw a venomous glance shot in her direction, mingled with a kind of covetous admiration, in a rather revolting combination, coming from such a source. It was at that moment that, for the first time, he had any adequate realization of the peril into which they had fallen—in which Fleda had fallen through his own folly, and her courageous loyalty to him.

It was in a mood of chivalrous desire to draw the malevolence that he had seen in Mr. Dancer's eyes in his own direction as much as to continue the good work of undermining his nervous system, that he replied: "I don't think I'd talk any more about that, if I were you. You're making poor Mr. Dancer go a very unhealthy colour. You mustn't forget that our friends here are all candidates for the same experience. Not that Mr. Dancer has much to fear, if he side-steps as quickly as a wise man would. Perhaps three months for car-

rying firearms without a licence, and then to be deported as an undesirable alien. It's Callaghan that's booked for the star turn. Though I
dare say he'll get off better than he deserves. It isn't prison he needs,
it's a dog's home. One of those where they're not kept more than
three days, unless some one calls."

While he talked on in this way, he was considering Mr. Dancer
in his more physical aspects. Not what the insurance companies
would call a good life. There were times when he coughed. But for
that damnable pistol, Basil felt that he could make short work of
him, in a way that Fleda could not fail to appreciate. Indeed, he had
little respect for the physique of any of the gang. Too much soft living. Too many cocktails and highballs. Tough enough at the start,
perhaps, but they'd been at it too long. If he could devise an instant's diversion, and a sudden spring? Suppose he pulled the cloth
towards him, as he had thought of doing when it bore Mr. Callaghan's pistol, and threw it quickly over his head? No, even his
buoyant temperament could not persuade him that there would be
time for that.

Then he had a better idea. There was a cross rail between the
front legs of the chair on which he sat, on which he had been putting
his right foot at intervals in the restlessness of that enforced inactivity. Suppose he got his foot firmly fixed there, and rose slightly, and
kicked it back with all his force against Mr. Dancer's legs? He
would need to have that gentleman directly behind him, which
would not be difficult, as he kept moving about between the door
and the chair-backs, and it would be best to choose a time when he
was having a good cough. The critical moment would be when he
swung round after the kick. However quickly he turned, there would
be an appreciable interval in which Dancer might recover himself
and fire, unless he were more or less knocked off his legs.

How hard would the chair strike? What would its effect be? It
was a novel method of attack, and he felt that even if he were free to
consult the whole literature of warfare and self-defence, it was improbable that he would discover any light upon it. Still it was his
duty to get Fleda out of this mess. It was worth a try.

And then, just as he was getting his instep firmly fixed on to the
rung of the chair, and composing a casual sentence which he must
be addressing to Fleda as Dancer got behind him, to throw him as
far as possible off his guard, the bedroom door opened, and Callaghan, with his cigar cocked up in his mouth at its highest angle,
and a general air of ruthless efficiency, led his retinue back into the
room.

CHAPTER XXVI.

WHEN Buddy Callaghan had seen that the intervening door was closed, and that what he was going to say could not be over-heard either by Dancer or those whom he had been left to guard, he sat down on the side of the bed, and addressed his followers.

"Boys," he said, "I've fetched you out here because I've got some good news for you that only came in on this mail, and because we're up against it good and plenty unless we do the right thing now. I'll give you the news first, and then we'll talk over how we're to deal with the rats in the next room."

He took from his pocket a sheet of the *New York Herald* eight days old, and passed it round. It announced, in the lurid headlines that are considered necessary to attract attention to anything in that blaring city, that the body of a woman which had been identified as that of the notorious Connie Blitz had been found in a thicket in Central Park. She had been shot in the back of the head, and must have died instantly. It stated that the police theory was that the mur-der had occurred elsewhere and the body subsequently thrown out from a passing car, and added that it had been rumoured for some weeks in the underworld to which she belonged, that she was a doomed woman, owing to her having double-crossed the well-known gangster Buddy Callaghan. It was said that she had declared that she was not afraid, and had threatened to shoot him at sight; and it recalled that she had been suspected of at least two previous mur-ders, but after being detained she had been released from lack of evidence in both cases. It added that Buddy Callaghan's name would have been almost certainly connected with the crime but that he was known to have crossed over to Europe some two months ago. The police were searching for the murderer with their usual diligence, and had already called up over thirty persons for examination.

Callaghan allowed a few minutes for the spirits of his followers to be raised by this satisfactory intelligence, and then addressed them with a confidence to which they were not accustomed, unless at an unusual emergency.

"Boys," he said, "we know that she'd got to go, and it wouldn't have done for me to have been about when she got what was coming to her, but Vitelli's kept his word, like the gentleman that we've always found him to be, and there's no reason we shouldn't go back now, just as soon as we can pack up, and I reckon by Saturday we ought to be out of this cursed country.

"There's only one thing that'll hold us here, and that won't either, if we can make this young Thornford choke up, and then treat him in the right way. I'd got that all fixed, till Dancer let that dame through, and if there's any paying to do for that we must leave him to settle the bill.

"Boys, if we don't get back the wad that was in my case, I shouldn't have a thousand bucks left when we'd checked out of here—"

He paused before the murmur of incredulous astonishment which this statement caused.

"Yes," he said, "I know what you thought, but it's no use meeting trouble before it comes. I sent over for all the cash I could need, but they've hung up paying the draft. They say they want more identification, and there's something else not quite O.K., and they've had to refer back to New York. Want another three weeks, and they guess it'll be put through. It's the cops here at the bottom of that. That's a sure guess.

"But we'll put one over them if we go back now, for we shan't need it here at all, and I shall just cancel the draft.

"But I mean to have that wad first. And it isn't only the dollars, or I might let it go at that, for a clear getaway, with this cop, Cleveland, smelling round as he is. It's the papers that were in that case, and though I don't ever risk much in that way, there's one or two there that'd just about light the match, if they spelled them out in the right way. The trouble in this country is that you can't tell where you can plant the graft for a good crop, or where the engine'll backfire in your own face. I got Jenks fixed for five hundred bucks, and there they were, all ready to be handed out, and he's not the man to squeal, and I'd got the cash in the case for the big deal. But it's no use talking of that now. We've got to have that case back, and if we can't get it friendly, we've got to have it the other way, and if we do that we've got to put them away, and perhaps Dancer'll come in handy for that. But there can't be anything coming out till we're safe on a U.S.A. boat, and nothing left lying round on which they can fetch us back.

"So you'll keep your mouths shut, and be quick to jump at the word, if you want to see Broadway again. And you'll leave me to tell Dancer as much as it's good for him to know, till I see how the cat jumps."

Devlin spoke for the first time. "There's always the stairs."

"Yes, but it's a chance that's too big at this time of day."

"Then I don't see—"

"You weren't asked." Buddy Callaghan stared at his lieutenant with his cigar at its most truculent angle. "Get that?"

Devlin said no more.

CHAPTER XXVII.

CALLAGHAN put down his cigar. He didn't trouble to pull out his pistol this time. He meant business, not show.

"Now, I've no more time to lose on you," he began, "so you'll do what you're told, without any more lip. You'll do it on the jump too, or you'll get hurt. You needn't talk about squealing afterwards, because we all know it's just what you wouldn't do. You'll make no noise about this, because you've no right to what you've got, and you won't make any more trouble, either. I've known a guy keep his jaw tight before now while the skin frizzled under his feet, but you're not that make. I reckon you don't want this dame of yours to spend the night here, and I reckon you want to walk out on your own feet. Well, if that's so, you'll get no five minutes now. You'll do it on the run. And I guess that's what you sure will. You've got the gab, but you haven't the guts to make any more trouble."

Fleda looked at Basil as this speech proceeded with questioning and anxious eyes. She wanted, very badly, to be out of this mess. She thought, with a confidence that may have been somewhat excessive, that she could have talked sense to Callaghan in a way that he would understand. But it was Basil who had to play his hand, and she was quite as anxious to see how he would come through as she was for her own safety. A familiarity with the criminal world from the friendly and yet aloof position of the legal office in which she worked may have given her an assurance which she would have cause to lose before the day ended, but for the moment she had only one thought. Callaghan's last phrase brought Mr. Morrison's verdict back to her mind. It was the same word, but which was right?

Basil could certainly talk. There was no doubt about that. Could he get out of the mess into which he had so impetuously fallen? Could he persuade or outwit? Would he bring her out with success, or would he buy her safety and his own with the surrender of all that he had at stake? She was not of the sort to wish that he should think only of her. She was not of a clinging kind. She saw that his dilemma was hard enough, but he had come here of his own will. If he went out defeated, they would both feel small enough. It would be a poor end to his boastful dreams.

She had a word at her tongue's end which might have helped, which might at least have delayed the issue, but she did not speak it. No one was looking at her. They were all watching to see what answer Basil would make. She wanted to know that too. She would sit back, and watch. Basil was brief for once. He said: "What do you want?"

"Where's my wallet now? In your room?"

"No."

"Then where is it?"

There was a moment's pause, at which Callaghan exclaimed impatiently: "Now then, spit it out."

"It's in the Porchester Safe Deposit."

"All there?"

"Almost all."

"How much?"

"There's the £5,000."

"All the papers?"

"Yes."

"You're sure of that? *All*?"

"There are all the papers, just as they were when I had it."

"That'll do. Then you'll give Mr. Devlin here the key, or whatever it needs to fetch it out, and if you've told the truth you'll be clear of this room in an hour's time."

"I won't do it that way."

"You'll do it the way you're told."

"If I give you the key, you'll let us go now? I couldn't get it without the key."

"Do you think we're just mugs? Have you got the key here?"

There was another short pause of hesitation, and then Basil gave a reluctant "Yes."

He brought it out, but still kept it in his own hand.

"It wouldn't be any use, without a signed letter from me."

"So that was the game? I didn't suppose it would. We're not that green in this racket. Dancer, pass the ink and some paper over here. You'll write that note now, and you'll write it the right way, if you want to get away with a whole skin."

"If I write it, we can go?"

"You won't go till Devlin's back, and I've seen that it's all here."

"But you can't keep us here like this. They'll—they'll be coming in to lay the tea."

"No, they won't. We're not Britishers here. We find we can eat enough at three meals. There'll be no one here for another couple of hours, and not then unless I call down."

"You can keep me till Mr. Devlin's comes back, and let Miss Collingwood go. That's a fair deal. I shouldn't offer that unless—"

Callaghan didn't answer this for a moment. He picked up his cigar, and pulled at it a time or two, as though considering the proposition. Then he said: "Get busy. That's agreed."

Basil might be excused if he believed him. The hesitation implied that he had only agreed after thinking that it could be done safely in that way. Besides, what choice had he but to trust? He could not see the falling eyelid of Smithers of the long tooth, who was standing behind his chair. Smithers had seen the Chief use that method before.

Basil wrote the note. Callaghan took it up, and read it carefully. He reached over for the key. He handed them both to Devlin.

"Don't lose any time," he said, "you'll find us all here when you get back."

Basil caught the accent of that "all," and a look of satiric humour in Callaghan's black eyes. He knew that he had been fooled.

Fleda made a movement to rise, but gave way to Callaghan's curt order, "Sit down, you." She laid a restraining hand on Basil's arm. "It's no use making a fuss now. It's too late for that."

CHAPTER XXVIII.

CALLAGHAN got up and walked into the next room. He looked round. Everything that mattered was packed away. He was a man who believed in keys. The door into the corridor was securely locked. They could do no harm there.

He came back. He looked at Basil with a cynical contempt. A poor lot these Britishers are when they come up against a real man. He had no thought for his Irish father, or his English birth. He said, "You go into the next room, you two. You can wait there. You give me a pain." The absurdity of the fellow trying to keep the cash, and hiding from place to place, and even going to Bletchworth & Co., and then absolutely walking into his arms in this way. Absolutely into his arms. He didn't even have to be fetched. But now that the thing was being settled without the trouble that he had wanted to avoid, without anything that might bring the police on to the scene, now that he could feel a comforting certainty that he would be clear of this hated country by Saturday, he wanted to talk, perhaps to boast a little to the hired companions who were the nearest to friends that such as he can ever know. He was his own confident, competent self again. For a time—it must be this cursed climate he had almost doubted himself. He forgot even his intention of not telling Dancer, in case it should be convenient to leave him behind. He abandoned his cautious plan of going back on an American line, so that he might be free at the earliest moment from the authority of the English flag. Why go on a ship on which they made it a favour to let you drink as you would?

"Smithers," he said, "ring up the Cunard. I want to know the best accommodation they've got, and tell them to have a clerk here at 10:30 with all the junk they want signed. Safe there? Yes, of course they're safe. There'll be no trouble from them. What'd be the use of making a row now? No, there's no phone in that room. You know that. I'm not going to have Rafferty ringing up so that I can't sleep. You can go into Devlin's room, one of you, if you like, and see if they try."

He grinned maliciously at the idea. It was one of his pet idiosyncrasies that he would have no line direct into his own bedroom. He preferred that Devlin's sleep should be disturbed by the calls which are liable to come through to such as he at any hour of the night. If it were really urgent, Devlin could let him know. When he had taken up his quarters at the Pelican he had at once ordered the change to be made. The instrument in his room went no further than to Devlin's bedside. It amused him to think of Basil ringing up the police-station or Mr. Morrison, or the safe deposit, and Smithers taking the call.

But Basil was not trying the instrument.

"I'm sorry," he was saying miserably, "I thought he'd have let you go. I only did it for that."

"You weren't asked."

There was an acidity in the tone which would have been unmistakable even to a more indifferent ear. This was something very different from the evening meeting of Basil's earlier imagination. They were alone, indeed, but the opportunity remained unutilized for the purpose which he had so plainly indicated. Neither did he offer to discuss the relative attractions of diamond or ruby rings. He only repeated: "I shouldn't have done it if I hadn't thought that he'd let you go."

"Considering what you *have* done," she replied bitterly, "I don't see why you should mind so much whether I leave this room at 4.30 or half-past five."

"That's because you don't understand."

Fleda looked at her miserable companion with a dawn of hope in her eyes. She thought that she had understood only too well. "Perhaps," she said reasonably, "if you explained, it would give me a better chance."

"Well—it's the wrong key!"

"The *wrong* key! Oh, Basil, and I thought you.... I can't say what I thought. I feel an absolute pig. And it looked like the right key. Hadn't it got the company's name on it? I thought I saw that when it lay on the table."

"Yes; Mr. Peters put me up to that, in case they tried the robbery-with-violence stunt, which he rather thought they would."

"Well, don't look so miserable about it. What do you suppose they'll say when Mr. Devlin walks in?"

"Haven't the foggiest. Try to ring me up here, or run him in, more likely than not."

Fleda Collingwood sat on the side of Mr. Callaghan's bed, with some indifference to its resulting appearance. She elevated her legs in an undignified and carefree way. She looked pleased at her own thoughts.

"I think you're going to alter the angle of that cigar."

But the look of worry or. Basil's face did not lift. "I shouldn't care," he said, with very probable truth, "if he'd let you go, as he said. It was a caddish thing to promise like that."

"And considering that you were giving him the wrong key! I don't think you've got overmuch to say."

"Yes. But what's he going to do when he finds out? It's all well enough about having known defeat and mocked it as we ran, and all that rot, but what about when you've got nowhere to run to? That's the song of lost endeavour that I make, and even a banjo couldn't make it sound much."

"Well, don't look so miserable. How long's he been gone? He can't be back for half an hour yet. More like an hour. That's if he ever comes. There's plenty of time to look through Mr. Buddy Callaghan's drawers, and get his spare pistols. Anybody'd think you *wanted* to be alone."

But Basil did not respond, even to that. He was thinking, as well as his wits allowed, of all the possible developments of the position in which they were placed, and how, if at all, he could get her out. He foresaw quite easily that when Callaghan realized the trick that had been played upon him he would be a very angry man. How he would act was less easy to decide.

He sat on a chair, at about three yards' distance from the girl whom he had destined both in imagination and correspondence for the immediate altar, and he dug his toes into the carpet in the extremity of his mental processes, appearing unaffected by her isolated proximity Into Fleda's mind there came a memory of Mary Daffern's critical eyes. She knew that she despised her technique. Certainly, Mary would not have been sitting thus, kicking up carefree heels, had she been in this dilemma. An impish spirit, born, perhaps, of the excitement of the hour, moved her to utterance. Did he think that their last moments had come? It was not exactly a case for a war-baby, but still, if so—

"Do you expect me to say, 'Come to my arms, my beamish boy,' or what is the required quotation in this instance?" she asked, in the voice of one who seeks guidance in an unexpected dilemma.

CHAPTER XXIX.

AT 2:00 A.M. on—yes, on Thursday morning—we have had occasion to notice already how early the next days begin when the week is advancing more rapidly than our plans for Saturday—Inspector Cleveland sat in the office of the manager of the Pelican Hotel, and received that gentleman's assurances as to the well-stocked condition of the coverts which he had come to draw.

Mr. Scarletti was in a condition of some excitement, and voluble as to the discretions and restraints of the previous day.

He said that Callaghan had come in shortly after lunch-time, and had stopped to buy some cigars at the counter, seeming in about his usual temper and spirits. He had then gone up to his own suite, with those of his companions who were with him, and from that time the whole gang had remained upstairs, except that Mr. Devlin had come down about four o'clock, and been away for about an hour. After that, there had been some noise in Callaghan's apartment, as though a quarrel had followed Mr. Devlin's return, which had been reported by one of the lift attendants, but, remembering his promise to the inspector, he had given orders that no one should interfere. Let them kill each other if they would. Nothing should occur to alarm them till the hour that the inspector had chosen. The disturbance could not have been very serious, for they had ordered dinner to be taken up at 7:30, when they had all been present, and appeared to be in good spirits, and their usual harmony.

He ought to mention that about 3:30 P.M. a young woman of attractive appearance (though not outraging the limits of respectability in that direction) had come in, and walked straight to the lift, asking to be taken to the third floor. The liftboy, not recognizing her as a guest, had watched her progress along the landing, and had seen her turn down the corridor leading to the Callaghan suite. He had not noticed more particularly, because his attention had been diverted by some people on that landing, who were in a hurry to descend. She had not been seen to leave, and might be still there. Of course, under more usual circumstances, he did not permit such incidents. Bed-rooms could be occupied only by those for whom they were taken, but remembering the inspector's instructions—

The inspector said he had done quite rightly. Was there no one else occupying any rooms on the same passage?

It appeared that there was only one, a young man named Thorn-ford, who came in during the afternoon, and had remained quietly in his room ever since. He had not answered his telephone, evidently wishing not to be disturbed, and the chambermaid, knowing that he was within, had respected his desire for solitude. No, certainly not a member of Callaghan's gang. A quiet, respectable youth. Good manners, but rather shy. Probably not stayed in a hotel previously.

Inspector Cleveland liked to do his business quietly and effi-ciently. He knew the reputations of the five whom he had come to arrest, and had brought three times that number, hoping to overawe resistance, even if he did not seize them in their sleep. He had a prison van waiting in a side street.

Silently and simultaneously the suite was surrounded and all its rooms were entered. So well was the surprise timed that the lights were switched on almost at the same second. The men would have wakened to lighted rooms, and to the muzzles of pistols levelled against their heads.

There was only one hitch in this programme, only one detail of deviation from its careful planning.

Callaghan and his gang were not there.

CHAPTER XXX.

INSPECTOR CLEVELAND had known quite well, when Mr. Scarletti was describing Basil, that he had not been one of the Callaghan gang. He knew who he was, and why he was there. But he had learnt to listen rather than speak. It is a point of wisdom at which most of us would arrive if we lived long enough, which few do.

When he found that the rooms of the Callaghan suite were empty, his first order to his subordinates was to examine the three other rooms in the corridor, and to request the young man occupying No. 337 to come to him as quickly as possible. He thought that Basil, even if his presence there had had nothing to do with their flight, might have valuable information to give him. He might, at least, have heard them leave.

He easily observed the line of retreat which had been taken by his escaped quarry. There were stairs there, for use in the event of fire, which ran up to the roof, and down to the ground floor.

Inspector Cleveland sent half a dozen men up to the roof to examine the position there. "But, if you see them," he said, "don't begin shooting, or do more than keep them in sight till you have let me know. We don't want any bloodshed about this, and the less publicity the better."

He sent for the manager also, who had kept well in the rear of these operations, and was quickly assured that it would have been impossible for the men to escape unseen from the lower end of the stairs.

But, before he saw him, he had learnt that Basil was also gone, and of the broken telephone in his room, and the information roused him to the fact that he might have to deal with a more serious issue than he had previously contemplated.

But he was too level-headed and experienced an officer to be flustered by the unexpected. He decided that he must follow his subordinates on to the tiles, and form his own judgment of the length and line of the flight that his quarry had taken. He decided also that he must speak to Mr. Morrison.

"Sergeant Gibbons," he said, "get through and report just what we have found. It seems to mean abduction, if not murder, though there are other possible explanations. It's too soon to say. But tell McClure to put every one on the lookout. He knows the men we're after. He'll know what to do. And get the best description of young Thornford you can from the staff here, and phone it through.

"When you've done that, get Mr. Morrison on the phone, and hold the line till I come back. If I'm not coming, I'll let you know." He hurried after his men.

The stairs opened on to the roof. The short summer night was fine but cloudy, and there was no moon. He found himself in a narrow gutter, with a low parapet on his left hand, and a sloping roof on his right. He could see down into the lighted street, but the diffused lights of the city made the level spaces of the roofs blacker than they would have been under the gloom of the night sky had there been darkness below. His men had gone out of sight or sound. He went on cautiously, with a ready gun in his hand, but as rapidly as the half-light permitted. He found that he could not only go the round of the hotel roof, but there were places—more than one or two—where an active man could easily cross to the adjoining buildings. As he returned to the head of the stairs he heard the sound of approaching steps.

"That you, Robb?"

"Yes, sir. We found where they got down. It's only a four-foot drop, and quite easy after that. But it might be any of forty houses this side of Belcher Street. They're just a straight row, with a dormer window to each. So I thought I'd better come back, and report."

"Quite right. But it may be more serious than it looked at first. There's a youth disappeared from an opposite room, and a broken phone, that looks like an effort to call help having been stopped."

"You'd better work along from window to window, and look for any signs of entering. Keep your ears open too, and if you see or hear anything suspicious don't hesitate to break in. But send a man back first to report. You'll soon have help, both above and below. And, Robb, tell your men to have their pistols ready. They're not after their own kind. They're the scum of New York. They'll shoot quicker than speak, if they think we're rounding them up."

He went back to the waiting group in the Callaghan suite, to be informed that Mr. Morrison was on the phone.

128

Mr. Morrison did not indulge himself in the sybaritic manner of Buddy Callaghan. He employed no deputy to receive the shocks of the night-calls which were a frequent feature of his legal activities. A telephone was beside his bed when he retired for the night at his pleasant Surbiton residence, and it was seldom that the operator needed to ring a second time before the receiver would be at his ear.

He had already learnt from Sergeant Gibbons that the police had missed their catch, and of the disappearance of Basil Thornford, and, when Inspector Cleveland came on to the end of the line, they were both of a better disposition to ask questions than to answer them.

"That you, Mr. Morrison? Well, you've heard that they've given us the slip. And this young Thornford's gone as well. Of course, if they've been up to any mischief with him, we shall have a clear charge, but, apart from that, I felt I'd like some assurance from you that the papers haven't given us the slip."

"I don't think you need worry about that—I don't understand about Thornford. A clerk from my office—a Miss Collingwood—went to the hotel to warn him during the afternoon. You might inquire on those lines. He may have gone out with her. That's the simplest solution. But, if not, I want to know—"

"If Thornford's all right—though he wasn't seen to go out, and I don't think he did—it makes it all the more important about those papers. You see, Mr. Morrison, we've been going entirely on your copies, and if the time came and you couldn't put the originals on the table we shouldn't be much better than public fools. I know bolting like this shows the funk they're in, but it isn't evidence of anything, standing alone. We might get a remand, on the strength of that, but we couldn't hope for more."

"I tell you that will be all right. What I want to know is—"

"Well, I suppose I must take your word. But them bolting like this shows that they're wise to the danger they're in, and if so—"

"What I keep asking is whether you'll find out if Miss Collingwood called, and—"

"There was a young woman who called between three and four. She didn't give her name. She went straight up to Callaghan's suite."

"And what then?"

"She wasn't seen to come down."

There was a moment's silence, and then Mr. Morrison's voice came again, with an anger which it did not often reveal: "If those swine—" It broke off, and resumed in a more usual tone, "You say they went by the roof. How does Belcher Street lie from there?"

"It's on the Belcher Street roofs that they went."

"Then just raid Number Thir—" His voice died into silence.

"Mr. Morrison. Are you there! I couldn't hear the number. You mean you know where they are?"

"Inspector," the voice had now resumed its normally slow and rather ponderous quality, "I can't give you that number, but just listen carefully. If they've interfered with one of our clerks you can reckon they're booked for the dock as surely as though you'd got the bracelets on them now. But I don't suppose five minutes will make any difference, and, if you want my help, you'll have to have it in my way.

"Yes, Mr. Morrison, that's always been understood, but—"

"Never mind the 'buts,' just listen to me. You needn't worry about the proofs. They're lying quite safely in the Porchester Safe Deposit in a pocketbook that once belonged to Buddy Callaghan. But there's some money in the case too, and it's not going to Scotland Yard. Most of it's for Mr. and Mrs. Thornford, and the balance is for Bletchworth & Co."

"We shouldn't care much what happened to Buddy Callaghan's money if we sent his gang where they belong."

"No, perhaps not. But if that money got into your safe, how do you suppose we should get it back?"

"I can't say that, not knowing—"

"No, nor I. So it just stays where it is. But I'm going to put a few more cards on the table than I have yet, and I'll tell you this. One of Callaghan's men called at the Safe Deposit this afternoon, with an authority from Basil Thornford to collect everything that was there."

"He didn't get it? Was that between four and five?"

"No, and yes. He didn't get it, because we'd had a little talk with the Safe Deposit yesterday. But that wasn't the only reason. He wouldn't have got it in any case, because he'd got the wrong key."

"You mean Thornford gave him the wrong key?"

"And why wasn't the man detained?"

"Inspector Cleveland! After you'd said you didn't want anything to happen to give the alarm!"

"Yes. I see. What did they do?"

"They said the key seemed to have been tampered with. And perhaps Mr. Thornford had better call himself in the morning, when they didn't think there'd be any difficulty. Something like that. I don't know exactly, but they sent the man off without any fuss, and rung us up to report."

"It rather looks as though Thornford fooled them over the key, and then stayed in his room a bit too long, and they dropped on him when they found out."

"Yes—more or less."

"What's the young lady's address?"

"It's 7, Hagen Road, Shepherd's Bush, and you'd better inquire, of course. But I doubt whether you'll find her there. She wouldn't have warned him, and gone off, and he been there a couple of hours afterwards."

"I don't quite see—"

"Then you can take it from me. She'd have taken that young man by the collar, and walked him out. And, if she hadn't, he'd have been at her heels."

"Then you think—"

"I think you'd better ring off, and you'll hear from me again within ten minutes. I may give you a useful address in Belcher Street."

The inspector put down the receiver. "Gibbons," he said, "have Number 13, and Numbers 30 to 39, Belcher Street, watched at once. And phone Vine Street for some more men. We look like making the catch, after all. But we'll need to have enough to secure the roof as well as the street."

He turned to give his own attention to a more thorough examination of the rooms than they had yet received, and had time to be puzzled by the fact that the luggage of the gang appeared to be in process of an orderly packing. There was no appearance of hurried flight, nor had there been the removal of such light or valuable or essential things as would most naturally be selected for a more leisured retreat.

"Sergeant," he said, "we couldn't charge them with bolting with intent to defraud. They've left too much behind. I almost think they meant to come back."

"Yes, sir. I was thinking that."

Meanwhile, Mr. Morrison was holding a conversation which it may be interesting to overhear.

"That you, Rafferty?"

"Yes, sir. I hope there's nothing wrong?"

"Nothing much. But you'll need to look out for a good house-agent."

"A good house agent?"

"Yes. For Number 36."

"You don't mean the police—?"

"No. But they will. Look here, man. Keep your head, and listen to me. I'm going to give them the address. No, of course not. With your consent."

Mr. Rafferty became incoherent in excited protest.

"Listen to me Rafferty. I told you to keep clear of Callaghan's gang. Well, the police want him now, and I want him too; and he's gone over the roofs, and in at Number 36. There's not much doubt about that. But there'll be nothing to worry you. They'll be looking for men, not goods."

"Yes, sir. It's all right, if you say so, as far as that goes. But they'll know where to look next time. You can't alter that."

"That's why I told you to look out for a good house agent."

"Yes, sir. I see. Can't you give me an hour to clear them out, or to find that they're not there?"

"Man, the street'll be half full of police. If you show your face there…. Listen to me. If I'm not wrong, Callaghan's got one of my clerks. No, a girl. Miss Collingwood. And, if any harm comes to her, he's going to fry in hell. That's his own phrase, and he's going to learn what it means. And while we're wasting time now, Cleveland may be finding his own way in, and where will you be then? Yes, that's a sensible man."

Mr. Morrison rang through to Inspector Cleveland again.

CHAPTER XXXI.

THE conversation between Basil and Fleda, so indecorously confined in Mr. Callaghan's bedroom, when we let the curtain of discretion fall and turned to the observation of incidents of a more conventional publicity, was not only of too intimate, it was also of too disjointed a character to be recorded in detail.

Conversational duets between men and women may be divided into three categories. They are those in which the woman constantly interrupts the man (which is the ordinary pattern), those in which they constantly interrupt each other, and those in which they interrupt each other and themselves also. The conversation which we have so discreetly avoided belonged emphatically to the last of these divisions.

If Basil tried to interrupt the ecstatic silence which is the language of initial physical contact to discuss the urgent problems of passports, churches, licences and rings (both gemmed and plain), he would find that he was interrupting himself to consider the still earlier urgency of the next interview with Mr. Buddy Callaghan; and, if Fleda replied in a natural effort to exhibit the absurdity of Basil's headlong plans, she would interrupt herself to suggest the possibility that such an interview might yet be avoided. At this emotional crisis of their inexperienced lives they did not merely interrupt themselves and each other, they interrupted their own interruptions continually. The conversation of Basil, complicated with the wisdom of Donne, Milton, Harriet Beecher Stowe, and several others, was particularly recondite, fragmentary and obscure and a proper sense of responsibility has forced me to the decision that, for the first twenty-five minutes after the moment when Miss Collingwood called Lewis Carroll to her shameless aid, it must be taken as read.

For that time, they had a feeling of temporary security. Devlin could not be back, and it was improbable in the interval that the gang would intrude further upon them. But as the minutes passed there was something which I should describe as a change of orientation, were I unreluctant to deviate from the simplicity of a chosen style.

Basil, hesitating upon Fleda's earlier suggestion that there might be a reserve of lethal weapons in Mr. Callaghan's private drawers, felt a scruple which we can understand without much difficulty in conducting such an investigation while the door might open at any moment, and their owner observe his occupation. He may have been deterred about equally by the thought that there wouldn't be anything useful to find. He credited Mr. Callaghan with too much sense.

He had more hope in investigating the window. It opened on to a four-sided well, with hotel windows all round it. The one immediately opposite to their own was of frosted glass, and its interior might be vacant. Still, a heavy object thrown through it might stimulate inquiry. He was right in thinking that such a breakage of glass would be sufficiently audible through any other open windows in that section to excite remark. Even the breaking of their own might serve the same purpose, if it were thoroughly done. His active mind suggested an even more promising method. He might tie a heavy object to a cord, let it down, give it a good swing, and break the window below. He imagined himself doing this, and Callaghan rushing in. "What the hell does that noise mean?" or something equally simple in expletive questioning. And he would reply, "There's nothing happening here. It sounds rather like trouble on the floor below." But he saw that he risked being defeated by his own subtlety. He might deceive not only Mr. Callaghan, but the hotel staff, and how much better off would they be?

Then he looked at a piece of rain-piping that ran down the wall about two feet away. Could he slide down it, and bring a glorious rescue to his bride-to-be? The answer might be in the affirmative, but he was not quite sure. He was not exactly afraid. He had a good head for heights, and was of a buoyant and adventurous mind. But he saw that, if he should arrive at the base of the pipe in a smashed heap, it would interfere with his plans for Saturday. He thought of "hostages to fortune," and "Felix, at what price we live," the application of which will be evident to all whose knowledge of our literature equals his own, which was quite moderate. He wished that some rehearsal were possible. If he were once on the pipe, he saw that it would be very difficult to get back. Still, perhaps it ought to be tried.

He called Fleda to the now open window, and announced his intention. She looked at him with some inward admiration for his daring, and at the depth below with a renewal of the conviction that he ought not to be out alone.

"Don't be such a donkey," she said reasonably. "Who do you suppose is going to get that money out of the safe-deposit when you've broken most of your bones there?"

He saw that. If he became a deceased (or was it a relict?) it would involve several complications. He suggested that he might make a will first. But he discovered, probably not for the last time, that Fleda knew too much law.

"Basil," she said, with the patience of a very recent affection, "don't be much sillier than you can't help. You'd need two witnesses for that. What do you suppose Callaghan'd say if you called him in?"

"I think you're making difficulties about nothing. A will made in expectation of immediate death doesn't need any witnesses. I read that somewhere. If a man is all alone in a boat, he has to write it on his own back in indelible ink, and the corpse has to be shipped home, and the lawyers shovel out the gold."

"I don't think you've got that quite right, and anyway it wouldn't do, because if you expect to get killed, and still do it, it shows you're out of your mind and the will's bad."

"Well, if you don't like my plan, what do you propose?"

"If you'd think less about getting out of this room, and more about other people not getting in—"

"I don't see what good that would do."

"Wouldn't five minutes be enough, if you used that telephone for the purpose for which nature intended it?"

Basil saw the idea. He remembered the expedient of the chair-back under the door-handle with which he had fortified himself in Miss Sporethought's apartment. He looked round for such weapons as that room had supplied. Alas, there was no water-jug here! He observed also, with a natural regret, that Mr. Callaghan removed his beard with a safety razor.

But he found a chair that fitted very well under the door handle. He decided that Fleda should be the one to phone. She would be out of the line of fire. He provided himself with a water-bottle for light artillery, and another chair for hand-to-hand fighting. He had a pleasant vision of Fleda at the telephone while he held the pass with whirling blows of the chair, his prostrate enemies thickly around his feet, while the rush of rescuers sounded along the corridor. Then the natural sequel of feminine gratitude, and a glorious, if somewhat, gory weeding.

"It's 'gang-plank up and in,' dear lass.
It's 'hausers warp her through'."

he remarked cheerfully, with a sequence of imaginations which a
little thought will interpret. "You phone, and I'll stand here."

It may occur to our cooler minds that there was no more probability of a telephone conversation being overheard than of that
which had been going on in that room for nearly half an hour, and
that there was no adequate occasion for such elaborate precaution.
That may be because, as Basil would have remarked, the looker-on
sees most of the game. Yet it may be observed that such defences
might have a simplifying convenience when the call for aid should
be answered in the expected way. If we imagine Mr. Callaghan's
dining-room entered by a hostile crowd and the retreat of the gang to
his own bedroom for a final stand, can we suppose that they would
get on with Basil and Fleda really well? No The Napoleonic mind
can be justified of that leaning chair.

Even apart from the idea of summoning aid by telephone, the
fortification had an aspect of the opportune, for, as Basil wedged the
chair, he was able to feel assured that the noise it made, and even an
unexpected rattling of the handle on both sides of the door that followed, would be unheard and unobserved, owing to the uproar
which broke out at that moment in the adjoining room, which we
must re-enter for its observation.

Mr. Devlin had returned some minutes earlier, but the murmur
of conversation that followed, deadened by the thickness of the intervening door, had been unnoticed by the preoccupied prisoners.
He had left the offices of the Safe Deposit Company, angry rather
than frightened, for the rebuff which he had received had been delivered in such a way as to avoid any suggestion of suspicion being
aroused. It was the wrong key, the clerk had told him in a friendly
and casual way, as though such incidents were of hourly occurrence.
To Mr. Devlin's first angry protest that it *couldn't* be the wrong key,
as though the clerk were himself in error, he had replied with apology, even as though he suffered from a similar doubt. He had even
suggested an explanation. Supposed Mr. Thornford rented two
safes—had two keys? Then, Mr. Devlin suggested, he could find
that out? No. Customers often rented two drawers in two different
names. No. He could make no inquiry. Customers' business was always treated as confidential. Absolutely. No offence to Mr. Devlin,

but if Mr. Thornford would come himself in the morning he was sure that everything would be to his satisfaction.

There was nothing to alarm Mr. Devlin in that conversation. His only feeling, as he re-entered his waiting taxi, was anger against the way in which, as he rightly guessed, Basil had fooled them deliberately. He thought with a savage pleasure of the probable results when Callaghan should be informed of this insolence.

But as he entered the hotel a different feeling predominated. Callaghan never was fair to failure. It was on himself that his anger would be first to fall. For Callaghan ruled by bullying, and by a sufficiently liberal distribution of the wealth which his methods won. Men had been driven instantly out of the gang, exiled from its rich rewards, for no worse a failure than must be reported here.

But it is seldom that the expected happens. Callaghan, biting savagely on his cigar, listened in ominous silence, from which no outbreak came. Curt questions clarified the narrative, concentrating upon the vital point—had suspicion been aroused, and would inquiry follow? He saw that he must guess the answer, and that he must guess it correctly if he were to be on the deck of the *Olympic* when Saturday morning came.

Such guesses were out of the routine of his peculiar activities, and he had become expert in judgment, and had learnt to act without vacillation upon a decision when it had once been formed. But here there was a disconcerting difference in the surrounding atmosphere. The Londoner is not easily comprehensible to the New York gangster. He allows himself to be disciplined by the police with a docility which has no parallel in the cities of the New World. He appears absolutely to like being regulated. He prefers the comforts and securities of slavery to the uncertainties and adventures of a freer world. If he were suddenly let loose in Victorian London he would feel as frightened of the undisciplined life as might a cage-freed bird that had been born in captivity.

The early Victorian could build his own house to his own plans. He could sell his own goods at 2:00 A.M. should he have any inclination to do so. They were barbarous times. He had the responsibility of spending almost all the money he earned, his rates being three and a penny and his income-tax three pence in the pound. It is a frightening thought. But even then the magic formula had been discovered which was to reduce him to servitude. He was to be told that he governed himself for his own good, and it was to prove the greatest instrument for bureaucratic tyranny, whether for good or evil, of which the world holds record. Even then the whips were cracking and the corralling process had commenced. Today he is one of a very timid flock, shepherded by the police, and fleeced by the tax-collector, whose death-duties will skin him clean at the end.

But this sheep-like attitude is curiously delusive, as Mr. Devlin had discovered when he proposed to alter the angle of Basil's arms. It was all very confusing to these men who came from a simpler land. What was the use of the six-shooter in your hip-pocket, if the surrounding population did not move in a perpetual readiness to erect its hands? If it did not whisper respectfully behind you, and give you wide space at the bar? Above all, what comfort or security could there be with a police of which you were never sure? Among whom it was known that there were men of very easy virtue, but so many of a more stupid kind that it was never safe to talk to them, as man to man, with a grand of bucks on the table?

Callaghan had only one feeling towards his native land. He wanted to leave it quickly, and he hoped never to see it again. If he could get away by Saturday, might it not be wiser to let the question of the pocketbook go, even with all it contained? However damning its contents might prove if they reached the hands of the police, and they could interpret them correctly, they would matter little if he were once away. Might there not be more risk in the endeavour to recover his property, in the short time remaining, than in leaving it to the hands of anyone to whom it might fall? It was not easy to say.

He knew that the attempt to establish satisfactory relations with Scotland Yard on a firm financial basis had failed. But he had given that up. If he were returning to New York, he had no reason to regret that failure. It was actually money saved—that is, if he could get it back. Otherwise, it would have been saved for Basil's benefit, not his.

He knew, from reliable sources of underworld information, that Inspector Cleveland was on his track. But, without the evidence in that case there was nothing that could be proved—nothing on which they would venture an arrest in this country. He was sure of that. He knew that the free and lawless way in which the police of New York will arrest and "hold" its citizens would be regarded as intolerable, even by the docile inhabitants of the Metropolitan area. It was true that they would sometimes make an arrest first, and rely upon a complacent magistrate to remand the prisoner while they collected the evidence, but they were careful not to do this unless they were sure that a respectable body of evidence could ultimately be produced. It was a method which would be quickly exposed and discredited by failure. No, apart from that pocketbook, he had really nothing to fear.

And the pocketbook was lying in the Porchester Safe Deposit, and he could, he supposed, have had it all back two days ago at a cost of £500 He had an unpleasant inward realization that he had been a fool. If he had only remembered that he was not in New York when Bletchworth's had rung him up! But he had answered on the spur of an angry moment, remembering that he was on the track of the young thief in his own way at the time.

He was of a stubborn, bullying kind, but he was not too obstinate to change his mind when the need was plain. He did not intend that anything should keep him longer in London. He would be gone by Saturday. And for that end he would make the best terms he could with his prisoners in the next room. He would give £500. Even more. But, till he got the pocketbook, he saw that he could not afford to let them go. He had gone too far. He had shown too much of his own hand. And they would be two witnesses against him. Through Dancer's folly. Two. No, he must hold them till he had the papers back in his own possession, and they had been paid whatever sum should be agreed, as the price of silence. Whatever risk there might be in holding them, it would be greater to let them go. The young woman might go straight to the police. Her own position was so clear. She had no responsibility for the retention of the pocketbook. She had been detained without justification. If she made any complaint it must all come out, including Devlin's visit to the Safe Deposit with the wrong key. He was not sure that he could not set up some amount of justification for his own conduct, but he was sure of one thing. When the police learnt that it was his pocketbook that was in question, they would contrive to have a sight of it on the way back to his hands. No, at this stage he could not let them go.

But he must make their detention as safe as possible, and he did not mean that it should be in his own rooms. The way was to come to terms with them first, so that they would be comparatively docile, and then transfer them to Rafferty's. If the absence of Basil from his room should lead to inquiry, or the young woman had been seen to enter, suspicion might point towards him at any moment, but if his suite were searched, and found to be vacant of them what more could be said or done?

Also, suppose that there should be such developments that it would not be safe to let them go till he were on the high seas? It would be impossible to leave them in the hotel rooms, and the transfer to Rafferty's might be more difficult at the last moment, and with them perhaps in a desperately hostile attitude by that time. He resolved that they must be moved that night. Placate first. Then move. Then deal with them as their conduct—and his own safety—might require. Had he been able to get his property back, at the cost of their lives, with a certainty of his own retreat, they would not have lived an hour; but, for the moment, whatever change might be coming, the risk of violence appeared too great. Like Mr. Stanley Baldwin, from whom he differed more or less in other respects, his motto was Safety First.

But he was not in the habit of taking his followers into a detailed confidence. He may have felt that he had done enough in that line already. He laid down his cigar, and said briefly: "Well, boys, I reckon he thought he was real smart, giving us the wrong key, and so he might have been if we'd let the dame go to sound the alarm. But here he is, and here he stays till I've got that case back where it belongs. I guess the right key isn't far off, and we'll soon know where it is, if it means stripping him to the skin." He did not expect any dissent.

He did not propose resolutions. He issued orders in that gang. Discussion there might be, or inquiry, if his orders were not understood; but when Dancer burst out with,

"You can't keep them like that. Not here. It isn't safe," his hard and angry stare had as much of genuine amazement as would that of a lion if one of his attendant jackals should dispute his prey. And from Dancer, who was the weakest, the most contemptible, the underdog of the gang!

But Dancer had the courage of panic. He had spent four years in one of the most merciless prisons of the Middle West, and had come out of it with damaged lungs and broken nerves, which he endeavoured to cover with such a front of courage as would enable him to maintain his place. The thought of honest living never entered his mind; and he felt a sense of protection, a confidence in crime, which he would have lacked alone, while he was a member of such a gang.

But this country gave him the jumps. Also, he had not the benefit of Callaghan's earlier confidences. His time had been spent in listening to Fleda's somewhat lurid portrayal of the rewards of iniquity as they are distributed in an English jail. For some hours, at the back of his mind, there had been a little lurking thought of something that he would never have the courage to do, but—*suppose he should*. It was a way of escape only possible in this alien land—only possible if he should resolve never to go back. He must stipulate with the police for that. That would be more important even than the reward which he felt sure that they would be prepared to pay. If he were afterwards expelled as an undesirable alien, and landed on the west side of Manhattan Island, how much mercy would there be for the betrayer of Callaghan's gang? How many hours of life before McClure's orders would issue, and some one would bump him off? No, he would never dare. But the thought had been there, all the same, and, though it might not grow to an active purpose, it was unwilling to die. It was as much an instinctive desire to save himself from a more acute temptation, as the fear that Callaghan's violent methods would prove the undoing of all of them, that had prompted that protesting cry.

Callaghan looked round, and saw that Dancer's fears were reflected in other eyes. It was not to one only that this country gave the jumps. He saw that if he failed to take a strong and confident line he would be the head of a broken gang. The nerves of such a gang have, as it were, a corporate individuality. The others cannot be confident while one member trembles. To put a bullet into him in such circumstances may be as necessary as the amputation of a gangrened limb. But a strong leader may remove a shaken *moral* by a display of his own confidence.

Callaghan knew all this well enough, but at that moment he saw more than the faltering of his follower's nerves. In an instant of sudden realization, he saw the full peril in which he stood. He saw that Dancer might squeal. It was a thought that could not have come to him in New York. He would have dismissed it there as too absurd for discussion. Dancer hadn't the pluck to put a bullet into his own brain, which it would surely do. Why, he had seen a hard-boiled gambler, who had held his own for seven years in Broadway's most lurid dens, go white at a mere baseless jesting remark that linked such a possibility with his own name. But in this country it was a different thing.

They were standing in a loosely formed group round the empty fireplace as Dancer made his protest; and, after one moment's pause of ominous silence, the storm burst.

Dancer drew back as Callaghan took a menacing step towards him. "Can't I?" he snarled. "And who made you the boss of this gang, you white-livered, crock-lunged, skunk-gutted dancing-master? Who got us all into this hell-damned mess by letting that dame through? There's one dancing-lesson you'll learn from me, and that's to dance to my tune. You'll keep your mouth shut till you're asked, and learn to run when you're told, as a dog should. *Take your hand from that knife.*"

It is improbable that Dancer's hand had gone towards the pocket that held his knife with any definite purpose. It was no more than the instinctive, frightened movement of a nerve-wrecked man, if it were even that. But he was the only one of the gang who carried a knife, and he was known to be very quick in its use. It was that celerity which had led to his detention in the penitentiary from which he had come out only three years ago.

Menace or not, its suggestion was the excuse for the blow that followed. Callaghan's fist drove hard and sudden to Dancer's chin. The man lay still where he dropped. Callaghan stood over him with a set jaw, but breathing rather hard from the exertion of that sudden activity. He was in poor condition, and would have made a sorry show in a sustained fight, but the single blow was given with the force of a piston, and no second was needed.

Callaghan looked round at his followers, and knew that he was their master again. He looked down with a sneer at the unconscious man. He knew him to be of a general unpopularity.

"Guess we're about through with him," he said, and then, with a slow deliberation, "If one of you boys thought he was going to squeal, you'd just put him quiet at the first chance, and we'd all see you through." He turned with the confidence of a renewed authority towards his bedroom door. "And now," he said, "we'll have them out. Smithers unlock that door."

It was just then that Basil had said, with a very natural satisfaction, "They seem to be having a little difference among themselves," and Fleda, who had shared his attention to the sound of Callaghan's angry voice, and the thud of the falling man, replied with an equal cheerfulness, "Their tempers ought to be good after this—perhaps it's time to try what the phone can do for us." And then they heard the key turn in the door.

They heard Smithers say, "The door's jammed," and then there was a moment's pause with no more than a murmur of voices from the other side.

Basil stood with the water-bottle in his hand He must throw it quickly when they burst in, to have time to pick up the chair, which would be his real weapon of defence. He did not hope to keep them out permanently, but to gain time for the rescue which Fleda would summon. Still, they couldn't all come through the door at once. "In that strait path a thousand might well be stopped by three," but unfortunately he was two less. Still, so were they. More so. If the arithmetic were good, he ought to be able to stop about three hundred and thirty. But perhaps Macaulay wasn't good at arithmetic. Or should Horatius take the blame? Anyhow, he'd got to do the best he could. He thought he could hit fairly hard with that chair. *Suppose he killed one of them?* How would he stand then? He had a well-grounded suspicion that it would interfere with his Saturday programme. It is difficult for anyone to hit at four or five angry men with a heavy chair sufficiently hard to distribute them over the carpet, and not too hard for them to get up again shortly afterwards. It needs practice, which he had never had. Even Horatius was unworried by the necessity of regulating his blows with such restrained precision. Still, if he did kill one of them, would it not be justifiable homicide? He wished there had been time to draw upon Fleda's fund of legal knowledge. They were illegally confined here by unprincipled and violent men, and in actual fear of their lives. It sounded all right up to that point. But why were they here at all? He had an unpleasant vision of himself in the dock, and a sarcastic counsel dwelling upon the significance of his numerous aliases. He saw the faces of the jury distinctly. They looked amused. He said aloud: "I'm not a lily."

"No?" Fleda replied. "Tell me about it another time. We're too busy now."

She was monotonously occupied in depressing the hook of the receiver, as per instructions, and in view of the surrounding circumstances it is not surprising that her temper suffered. There is an old tale of a useless passenger who worried the captain of a storm-beaten ship to let him help, until the exasperated man tied a rope to the binnacle, or the sheer strakes, or the studding-sails, or something equally useful, and told him to pull at that, which he did till the storm ceased. Captain and passenger may have passed away, but a postmaster-general must have read the tale, and how many hundreds of millions have moved the hook slowly up and down, in consequence, to keep them happy while the operator has gone to supper?

Basil realized that it was hardly the moment for a quiet chat. The handle rattled again. The moment for action was upon him. Well, it was no use letting I dare not wait upon I would, or being willing to wound and yet afraid to strike, he must be stern to inflict now and, if necessary, stubborn to endure afterwards.

"Open the door, you young fool." It was Callaghan's genial voice. And then, "Force it, Flipps."

The door gave way an inch or two—sufficiently to remain unlatched as the pressure slackened. It occurred to Basil, as he watched, that he might have blocked it with more substantial furniture. But it was too late to think of that now. Some one charged the door heavily. Beneath the shock, a leg snapped. The chair slid along the floor for a few inches, and then held again, on three legs. Basil hurled the water-bottle at a head which showed in the gap of the opening door. The bottle reduced itself against the side of Mr. Flipps's head, and its remaining portion went on to smash loudly on the central table. Basil picked up the chair.

There was a moment's pause, punctuated by the curses of Mr. Flipps on the other side of the door. Fleda stopped saying, "Are you there?" and lifted considering eyes to the impending conflict. There were five men on the other side of that yielding door. She did not know that Dancer was off the list for the time. She decided that there could be only one end.

"Basil," she said, "let the gentlemen in. It's a dud phone."

A voice sounded behind them. Callaghan's voice. "Sure that's a bum guess." They looked round startled. He had entered unheard by the door from the passage. He did not look exactly kindly, but in an excellent humour. He chuckled audibly as he locked the door on the inside and put the key in his pocket. He had a gun in his hand, but it was a demonstration of force rather than a threat of any active hostility.

"Don't trouble to let them in. I want a little talk with you two," he went on, in a tone that approached as near to geniality as he could easily manage.

Basil, with some reluctance, put down the chair. He crossed over to Fleda, who occupied the one by the bedside telephone-table. As he did so, he had a glimpse of the further room, through the gap of the partly opened door. Flipps mopped a bleeding ear. Dancer was sitting up on the floor.

Basil sat by Fleda on the bedside. Callaghan put the pistol back in his pocket. He took the only remaining vacant and uninjured chair. He said: "Do you two want a job?"

They both appreciated the change of atmosphere from the shadow of sanguinary conflict which had been upon them thirty seconds before. They felt almost inclined to forgive Mr. Callaghan this uninvited intrusion into his own room. But it was hardly a position which disposed them to say "Yes," together, and produce their references.

Basil was the first to answer. He combined politeness with the pursuit of his main objective, the accustoming of Fleda to her approaching fate. He said: "Not at the moment. You see, we're getting married on Saturday."

Fleda looked at him with something in her eyes which even he could not misinterpret as a meek submission, though its amusement might be either of an affirmative or negative character. It was hard to tell. But, however that was, she decided after a moment's silence that she must back him up. They weren't going to dispute about before Buddy Callaghan.

"You see," she said, "we shall be going abroad for a few weeks, if not more. Perhaps, when we come back, if you'd anything very attractive to offer, Mr. Thornford might—"

Callaghan interrupted, "Where to?"

"We hadn't quite decided that. I wondered whether you could tell us if it would be too hot in New York at this time of year?"

"New York? You going there? That's sure fine. Too hot? Not a bit. Now look here, baby"—he drew his chair nearer to Fleda, and his black eyes admired her eloquently—"you tell your boy to just come along with me. I'm sailing for N'York on Saturday too. He's a smart guy, and the two of you could pull off things that I couldn't try with this bunch." He waved a contemptuous cigar, which he had taken out but not yet lighted, towards the half-open door. "It'll be five grand a year each, and ten per cent beyond that every time that we make a kill."

This was a new Callaghan. Ingratiating, almost oily in manner. Indescribably repulsive to Basil, as he pulled his chair a few inches nearer to Fleda, who actually did not seem to mind. She was looking at Callaghan with that amused, considering glance that he had learnt to love (but not directed as it was now!) and appeared unconscious of his own sulky silence.

"Don't you think," she asked, "we'd better settle one thing at a time?"

"You'll find we've settled the lot, if we settle this in the right way."

"But we couldn't settle it straight off. We should have to talk it over together."

Callaghan was a good negotiator on his own lines. He looked at Basil, who didn't look really pleased. He judged that, if his proposal were to be accepted, it would be because Miss Collingwood knew her own mind and Basil's too. He would gain nothing by pressing for a reply now. Besides, it was not his main objective to secure their consent, though it was a quite genuine offer. They would be recruits worth having. And the fact that they might travel out on the same boat as a newly wedded English couple who, of course, did not know him at all, might provide immediate opportunities of making

profit in the peculiar ways in which he specialized so successfully.
Also, it would simplify everything. The money and papers would be
recovered. The legal difficulties that might otherwise arise from
their somewhat irregular detention would disappear. But it was useless to press for a decision now. A refusal, or insincere acceptance,
would not help him at all. Many times his business had taught him
the folly of digging up a seed to see whether it were taking root. He
said easily: "Take your own time about that, though there's hundreds that wouldn't think twice if they got that sort of offer from
Buddy Callaghan. Hundreds with bigger wads in their wallets than
maybe you've ever seen. But now on this little matter that's brought
us together here. You've played a dirty card on me with that key,
and I might take it the wrong way, as most would, but we'll let that
be."

"Only, don't try it again. I'm going to offer you what ought to
leave us all friends, and I mean it straight if you play the game in the
same way. You're going free out of here, and you'll get your ten per
cent and a bit more. You'll stay here for the night, or a few doors
off, and you'll come to no harm, and tomorrow morning"—he
turned to Basil as he said his, and something of the menacing trucu-
lence that was his more natural manner came back with the words—
"you'll go with Devlin, and get that pocketbook, and you'll send it
back here—you needn't come back yourself, if you don't want—and
if I find it's got my papers just as they were, and four thousand five
hundred pounds, I shan't ask where the other five hundred is, nor the
smaller notes, though there was enough of them to make it a good
day's work for you when you lost your own. And, if you don't want,
you needn't see me again till we meet on the ship's deck; and, if you
want a job, then you can come to my suite, and we'll have a little
talk there."

Basil pondered this in a very sceptical mind. He was not only
sure that he did not like Mr. Callaghan. He had disliked him from
the first, but it was only when he talked to Fleda in that familiar way
that he fully realized how objectionable he really was. That was the
real point—Fleda. He said: "You haven't mentioned Miss Collingwood. If you'll let her go now—"

"Miss Collingwood will be free to leave as soon as Devlin gets
back."

"That's the sort of thing you promised before."

"You'd better not say too much about that. If I'd been fool
enough to trust you over that key, I'm not trusting you now. Miss

Collingwood leaves when the case is here. And there'll be no tricks this time, if you're a wise guy. Not if you want to see her again."

"You wouldn't dare—"

"You'll find that out, if you try."

"Anyhow, I'm not going to leave her here."

"You young fool! What use would it be to keep her, if I've got back what I want?"

"Well, I shan't—"

"Yes, Basil, you will," Fleda interrupted coolly, "it's a very fair bargain, I think, and shows we both trust each other just as far as we can be expected to do. And, as soon as you've given Mr. Devlin what you've agreed, I'd like you to phone Mr. Morrison and say I've been detained, but I'll be at the office in about twenty minutes."

"I don't see how I can trust—" Basil began.

Fleda interrupted again.

"You're not asked to trust anyone. I'm the only one that does that, and I'm trusting you."

"I don't see that."

"Then you're not trying very hard. I'm trusting you to send back four thousand five hundred pounds. If you go off with it, as you can if you like, where does it leave me?"

"You know I shouldn't do that."

"Yes. I said I was trusting you, didn't I? But that's all the trusting there's going to be in this deal. Mr. Callaghan won't want me on his hands when he's got his goods back, or any more trouble on that score. He'll just want to forget."

Fleda spoke from a somewhat exceptional knowledge of the methods of the illicit transactions of the underworld, with which the business of her firm so largely dealt. She recognized in the details of the present proposal that Buddy Callaghan was a mastermind in his own line. She was sure that Basil would not fail to return the money to secure her liberty, and Callaghan must have come to the same conclusion. She saw that he had also offered terms sufficiently liberal to make it unlikely that there would be any serious trouble during the night about their detention, or afterwards when they were free with the best part of a thousand pounds in their pockets.

It had occurred to her earlier that what Mr. Callaghan really needed was the services of a good firm of solicitors, and she had considered the expediency of producing the business card of her firm as a peace-offering at more than one critical moment. It was true that they were already acting for Basil, and true also that Mr. Morrison made it a rule that he did not allow any professional blackmailer to benefit from the resources of his legal knowledge, but she thought that both of these difficulties might have been overcome. But now she changed her mind, considering that Mr. Callaghan was well able to look after himself. She only said, as Basil continued to stare at the carpet in a moody silence: "But there's one thing I hope you won't forget, Mr. Callaghan, and that is that we're not accustomed to having only three meals a day. We've had two, and it's nearly time for the fourth, so you can judge how we're feeling now. But if you'll call down for a good meal, and there aren't any fleas in the beds next door, or wherever it is, I don't see why we need look as though we'd just lost a couple of favourite aunts, if not more."

But Basil did not respond to this flippancy. He continued to survey the carpet in unresponsive gloom.

Mr. Callaghan had no intention of starving his compulsory guests. But neither did he intend to announce their presence to the hotel staff. He said he'd have a good meal served as soon as the dinner-hour approached, and when the room had been straightened.

With the keys of both the outer doors in his own pocket, he superintended the removal of all signs of the recent disturbance. Every scrap of glass must be picked up. The marks of Mr. Flipps's blood, which had been rather freely distributed, must be removed. That gentleman must retire to his own room to continue his ministrations to his still-bleeding ear. Disordered clothing must be reduced to its usual decorum. Basil and Fleda must be locked again in his bedroom, and must pledge themselves that there would be no sign of their existence when the waiters came. On that condition, they should be assured of an ample meal. It was a promise willingly, even eagerly, made, and punctiliously observed; and the meal which followed, though somewhat irregular in the intervals and vehicles of its transmission to Mr. Callaghan's bedroom, was ample and satisfactory enough to render it difficult for Basil to continue to forecast the future under darkened skies.

CHAPTER XXXII.

"How," Miss Collingwood inquired, "do you expect me to continue to smile at Mr. Smithers every time he comes in if you go on there as cheerfully as Jonah sitting under a gourd? And if I don't continue to smile at Mr. Smithers, how can we be sure that he'll go back and fetch it every time he forgets the salt?"

"I don't care a damn about the salt," Basil replied, with what was for him an unusual display of temper, as well as extremity of expression. "I don't care a damn about it, unless you know how to put it on that bounder's tail."

"Basil," Fleda replied coldly, "when you talk like that, you make me wish I'd married you years ago. Think what I've missed."

"Well, if you can't see for yourself—"

"You must make allowances for the limitations of the female mind. If I can't see something, why not say it in simple words?"

"Well, I should have thought you could."

"I suppose you'll take my word for my incapacity?"

"We've got to agree to be tied all night by the leg—"

"My company being so particularly unpleasant?"

"You know I didn't mean that. And I don't suppose I shall have it, either. Not all night, that is. I don't know what he'll contrive."

"Basil," Fleda replied, in an ominously quiet voice, "I'm rather good at taking care of myself. You needn't trouble about me."

"You know I didn't mean that, either."

"What did you mean?"

"Anything you wouldn't want me to. It isn't only being stuck here, or somewhere worse during the night, with the money in the next room, it's what might happen tomorrow, if—"

"What money in the next room?"

"All the lot that's coming to us, except the five hundred pound note."

"Well, there's not much in that. You can get it after."

"Suppose they give the room to some one else? They'd find the money for sure when they put it straight."

"Basil! You don't think they take the carpet up every time the room has a new guest?"

"I don't know, but they might."

"They might repaper the room. Even if they did find them, you'd get them back."

"If I could prove they were mine. I wonder how I'd do that."

"Yes; there is that. But I don't think there's much to worry about, all the same. They won't find them. And they won't let the room to anyone else, because you haven't given it up. Your luggage is still there, isn't it?"

"Yes."

"Then I think you're making a great fuss about next to nothing at all."

"It isn't about that."

"Then why say it is?"

"I didn't. It's the way you kept interrupting."

"Well, go on. Let's know the worst."

"Suppose they won't give me the pocketbook? How would you be then, whether I come back or not? He wouldn't be doing it this way, if he hadn't something a bit more difficult than a room next door."

"Basil, I thought of that all by myself. I really did. That's why I said I'm the only one who's doing any trusting in this deal, and I trust you. But of course you'll get the case. Why shouldn't you?"

"If the police don't interfere, after what's happened this afternoon."

"I don't see why they should. Not against you getting it out, anyhow. But if there *should* be any muddle, you'd better go straight to Mr. Morrison, and get him to telephone Callaghan, if possible before Devlin gets back. If Mr. Morrison's out, tell Peters, and just leave it to him. Is that all?"

"It would be quite enough, if it were. But it isn't only that. It's the way we're wasting the time. And I've got to see Ethel at eleven."

"Ethel? I don't think I've heard of her. Is she another lady you're marrying at the weekend?"

"No, of course not. But that isn't all. It's how to get at the key."

Fleda saw that she might be coming to a real difficulty at last. She postponed inquiry as to the identity of the mysterious Ethel, to reply in a kinder voice: "If you'll tell me what the trouble really is, I dare say we can help each other to think of a way out."

"It's with the money in the next room."

"That is a bit awkward. Still, I don't know, but—Basil," the last word came in a suddenly softened voice, "are you really serious about Saturday?"

"*Am I...?*" Words failed before the sudden hope which the tone and the question brought.

"Because, if you are, and if you can pull it off—there really will be a good deal to do—it's what Mr. Callaghan calls a deal. Basil, don't...*don't*...! Anyone might come in any minute. Besides, I'm not doing it for you. Not in the least. It's because some one bet me a hat."

CHAPTER XXXIII.

IT was 1:30 A.M. on Thursday morning when Callaghan led the way to the fire-escape stairs. The corridors of the Pelican Hotel are lighted through out the night, and there is no hour at which its guests may not be coming in from some revel of the dark hours or issue forth for such purposes as may be left unquestioned. But, even in the Pelican, people must sleep, and the night is the most natural and the most usual time for that occupation. As there were no other guests located along the passage on which Callaghan's suite opened, the chance that anyone would observe them was remote indeed.

He led the way, followed by Flipps and Smithers. Basil and Fleda came next. They had given their words that there would be no attempt either at escape or alarm, as a condition of the next morning's bargain, and they had heard Callaghan's orders that they were to be shot down without mercy should they attempt to make trouble of any kind. Devlin and Dancer came behind. Callaghan did not bring the whole gang as a necessary guard so much as that they should all be involved in an equal responsibility. He meant to be back in an hour, and get as much sleep as he could in what would be left of the shortened night.

They made their way quietly and easily enough over the shadowy roofs, stooping as they passed the dormer-windows of the Belcher Street houses lest their forms should be visible to any who might lie awake in those attic-rooms, and so came to the one which gave entrance to No. 36, where Rafferty, prince of pickpockets and one of the most wholesale receivers in London, was believed by Mr. Morrison to keep his secret store.

Here Callaghan advanced alone, ordering the rest to stay some five or six yards behind, so that they were unable to tell by what means he signalled to whoever might be within, but after some time of waiting there was a sound of low voices, Callaghan's with an increasing impatience against the protests that met it, until it rose incautiously and the words came clearly, "unless you want the street roused," and "then be quick and let us in."

The next moment he called to them to come on, and one by one they stepped through the dormer-window, to a floor about two feet lower, and stood in a dark and empty attic, where they were left without light for about ten minutes, when their unwilling host returned, with a candle in his hand.

Callaghan spoke to Fleda with as much civility as he had available for ordinary occasions. "This," he said, "is Mr. Ormerod. He will make you as comfortable as he can for the night."

The name was new to Fleda, which was her first disappointment. She looked at its owner, and had a second. She did not know—was, indeed, sure that she had never seen him before. She was almost surprised at this, as so many of the criminal population of London occupied seats, sooner or later, in Bletchworth & Co's. waiting room.

She was even more surprised at Mr. Ormerod's appearance. He did not look like a criminal to her experienced eyes. A small, elderly man, neatly dressed, even in the hurry of the last ten minutes Highly respectable. Normally of a rather fussy but kindly disposition. Now anxious and worried. So she would have judged him. Probably rather old-fashioned in his views and habits. The small grey tuft of neatly-pointed beard was evidence of a precise disposition, and of the traditions of a past generation.

Mr. Ormerod raised the candle in her direction. His scrutiny of her may have been as keen as her own. He said: "If you will follow me, Miss—"

"Collingwood, of Bletchworth & Co., solicitors," she interjected pleasantly, as he paused at the name.

She had the satisfaction of seeing a startled flicker of Mr. Ormerod's eyes. But he went on smoothly: "Collingwood. My daughter will do her best to make you comfortable, as far as circumstances permit. Our accommodation is very limited. I'm afraid she'll have to ask you to share her room."

He spoke so naturally, with such a note of sincere apology in his voice, that Fleda felt her intrusion almost as though it were a personal rudeness.

"I'm sure I shall be quite comfortable," she answered. "I'm afraid we've made rather a late call."

She followed Mr. Ormerod down steep and narrow uncarpeted stairs, with a door at the foot that opened on to a square landing, Callaghan's heavy tread sounding behind them.

He had ordered the others to wait in the unlighted attic, where Basil found himself standing by the dormer-window. Could a sudden blow disable Smithers, who half-blocked the narrow exit? A sudden scramble get him through the casement, and out on to the freedom of the shadowy roofs? He was restless for action, anxious to do something to demonstrate his capacity, feeling that his Napoleonic qualities had been insufficiently demonstrated since Fleda had walked into Mr. Callaghan's dining-room. But it was, at best, a precarious chance, which would leave her isolated and in their enemies' hands, if it succeeded, and the position much worse if it should fail. Till the morning, at least, it might be best to fall in quietly with their captors' plans. There was still the question of how he should get back to his own room, without the escort of others, so that he might recover the key without disclosing the money to a very probable cupidity. That required a soothed and complacent Callaghan, rather than one who had been angered by an abortive effort to escape. No, a reluctant prudence restrained him.

Meanwhile, on the landing below, Mr. Ormerod, candle in hand, had turned and faced his unexpected guest. He addressed her with something of the manner of a determined sheep, and avoiding Callaghan's scowling eyes.

"Miss Collingwood, I should like to have your assurance that you are here of your own will—that you are not being detained?"

Fleda paused, and there was an atmosphere of silent tension, which she saw might break into storm—but to what end?—should she reply in an unsatisfactory way. She remembered her decision to carry through on the lines of the bargain which had been made. She gave him a smiling reply, her eyes going on to the dressing-gowned figure of Miss Ormerod, now standing in the opening of her bedroom door.

"No, it's too late to go home now. I shall be very glad if it's not inconveniencing you too much. Of course, I shall want to get back to the office tomorrow."

She went in with Miss Ormerod to a room that was neatly and plainly furnished in an old-fashioned way, with a large illuminated text, on which her eyes first fell, *Thou God seest me*, over the bed.

Callaghan's angry growl burst out as the door closed. He had put a bullet through many a man for less than that. So he said, but Mr. Ormerod looked at him with a timid firmness.

"I'm not in this, Mr. Callaghan, and I don't mean to be. But I don't see why you complain. That question may have saved you five years."

Callaghan turned without further words, and went back to his waiting followers.

"Devlin," he said, "you'll stay here with Thornford till morning. You won't come back to the hotel till you've been to the Safe Deposit, and brought back what's agreed. Thornford can come back with you, if he likes. Half an hour after that, he can meet Miss Collingwood at the hotel, or anywhere else, except here." He turned to Basil, to say with a sudden curtness, "You'll forget this place, if you're wise. And Miss Collingwood won't be here then. We're not mugs. But, if you do your part, there'll be no harm come to her." He spoke to Devlin again. "You won't sleep till this job's over. Thornford can, if he likes. And you'll keep your gun handy. I'll see you through if you shoot, but not if he gets away. If he did that, there'd be no place left for you in my gang." Once again Basil had the benefit of his eyes. "You'll understand, when I talk like that, it doesn't mean anything. We've made our deal, and we're all friends now. But it's only business to make sure."

He went back up the attic stairs. He felt he had done the job. It wouldn't do for Basil to get away, and perhaps give an alarm, while Miss Collingwood was in that house. Afterwards, if he gave Devlin the slip in the open street—well, she wouldn't be so easy to find. But he didn't think that he'd try anything of the kind. Basil wouldn't want to go to the police much more than he did himself. No, he had brought the job to a good end, as he always did, and by Saturday he would be on the way back to a city where he could walk down Broadway (should he condescend to the use of his own legs) with the pleasant feeling of being recognized for the power he was. Meanwhile, he would return to the hotel, and have a drink, and get to bed....

Smithers put his hand on his arm in the darkness as he reached the top of the stairs. "*Hush,*" he whispered, "*cops on the roof.*"

"*Cops?* Nonsense. It must be some of Rafferty's gang."

"There's half a dozen cops, if not more, passed the window two minutes back. They shone a light in, but they didn't see anything. We were lying close under the window. They may be coming back now."

Callaghan found it hard to believe. What should bring them here? An hour ago it had been no more than a thought in his own mind that he would bring Basil and Fleda. Everything had been quiet in the hotel when they left their rooms. It had been so smoothly done. It seemed absurd that half a dozen policemen should be on their tracks over the roofs.

Yet it might be true, and it was not a question to argue now, if it were.

"Window closed?"

"No. Not fastened. There wasn't time."

"Then bolt it now, and no noise. And then come after me."

He went down at once. If it were true, and the cops had come, and found his rooms empty, there might be trouble enough. Still, it was better than having been there at the time. And if he had half an hour now he might still give them the slip. And he ought to have time enough. The dormer-window had a solid frame, and some good bolts. They wouldn't break it unless they were quite sure. And, at the worst, the boys must use their guns. But they might not be after him, even if they came here. It might be Rafferty's racket, and he just butted in at a bad hour. Or could that young Thornford have got out an S.O.S.? There'd be a bullet to spare for him if he thought that, though it were the last in the gun.

CHAPTER XXXIV.

INSPECTOR CLEVELAND had used the interval, while he was waiting for Mr. Morrison to phone him the required address, in making a rapid but very competent examination of the Callaghan suite and of Basil's room. Not being descended from Mr. Sherlock Holmes in the direct line, he did not observe that several specks of dust at the side of Basil's bed had been turned over, and were exposing a fresh side, in such a way as to indicate that a young man not much over twenty had crawled under it about eleven hours earlier. In consequence of this obtuseness, which is characteristic of the official mind, he failed to discover the key and banknotes which we know to have been under the carpet. But he satisfied himself that, apart from the evidence of the broken telephone, there were no indications of any struggle having taken place in that room, and his prosaic mind recognized that the condition of the instrument did not imply that any personal violence had occurred.

He looked more seriously at a slight smear of blood on the side of the basin in the bedroom which should have been occupied by Mr. Flipps, and the badly cracked condition of a chair leg in that of Mr. Callaghan, which had been carefully straightened, but which was discovered by the keen eyes of Sergeant Gibbons, had an equally sinister complexion. He looked round the room thoughtfully.

"I wonder," he said, after a few silent moments, "what has become of the water-bottle?"

"Looks like a bit of it here, sir," P.C. Hetherington called through the open door. He pointed to a little sparkle of glass in the dining-room carpet.

Inspector Cleveland felt that he was occupied in a very interesting night's work.

Then the telephone bell rang again, and Mr. Morrison came through. He listened for a time, and then said: "Yes. That's agreed. We're looking for men, not goods. Rafferty's clear out of this, if he isn't in it himself. You understand what I mean. Tell him to go to sleep. Yes. Number 36. Thanks. I won't forget it." He rang off hastily.

"Now, Gibbons," he said. "There's to be no mistake about this. Your men have all got their guns. They're to watch the window of Number 36, Belcher Street, and arrest anyone who tries to get out. They're not to hesitate to shoot, if there's any threat of resistance. But if no one comes out they're not to expose themselves before the window, nor to try to break in, unless they hear shooting inside the house, and then they can't be too quick. I'm going down to the street. I shall get some men round to the back first, and then go up to the front door. We can't break in till we've given them a chance to open in the right way. If you're in doubt as to which the house is, we'll signal from the street. It ought to be the eighteenth from this end."

It was a quarter of an hour later that he knocked at Mr. Ormerod's door. It belonged to one of a row of high, narrow, monotonous houses of a gloomy respectability, now dark and silent, as such houses usually are in the midnight hours. Three of his subordinates stood behind him, and others watched at short distances.

He knocked three times at intervals with an increasing vehemence, and then heard a faint sound through the slit of the letter-box. Some one was coming down the stairs.

The door opened a few inches, and Mr. Ormerod, now in a dressing-gown, with a candle in his hand, looked out. Inspector Cleveland put his foot into the gap. He might have pushed it further open, but the chain held.

"What do you want, knocking me up at this hour?" Mr. Ormerod demanded with mild severity. "Oh, I beg your pardon, officer. I didn't know it was the police. I hope there isn't anything wrong?"

"Be good enough to open the door, and I'll tell you then. We're looking for some men that you're believed to be harbouring here."

"Men here?" Mr. Ormerod looked his astonishment. "There's no one but myself and my daughter in the whole house."

"That's what I've got to find out."

Mr. Ormerod took off the chain. "You'd better come in."

He led the inspector to an adjoining room. He went in alone, leaving his men at the door. He did not know what was before him, and his instinct was to proceed cautiously, but he showed no lack of courage as he followed Mr. Ormerod's candle singly through the shadows of the house which was probably occupied by five armed and lawless and possibly desperate men.

Mr. Ormerod lit the gas.

"I'm afraid," he said, "you'll think we're rather old-fashioned, but I never have taken to electric light. It seems so glaring to me, besides being rather dangerous, and I believe it's a lot dearer than gas."

The inspector declined to be led into discussion of the merits of various means of illumination.

"You'll understand, Mr.—thanks, Ormerod—that I shouldn't have come here without serious reason. I have good cause to believe that a party of five American gangsters have taken shelter in this house, either with or without a young man and woman who have disappeared under rather strange circumstances. If I am correct, you will be acting very wisely if you give them up; in which case, as far as my present information goes, you will have nothing to fear from us."

"I think, Inspector, you must have come to the wrong address. I can assure you that there is no living person in this house except my daughter and myself."

"Then, if you can't or won't tell me anything more, I must look for myself."

"I have told you that you are making a very serious error. I strongly object to having my house disturbed at this hour. I should particularly object to any intrusion into my daughter's room."

"I am sorry, Mr. Ormerod. But I have my duty to do."

"Have you a warrant to search my house?"

"No, I have not."

"Then I refuse my permission."

"Listen to me, Mr. Ormerod. There are about fifty of my men surrounding this house. I may be right or wrong, but I have information on which, warrant or no warrant, I am bound to act. You needn't say anything to incriminate yourself, but you can just listen to me.

"Quite apart from this trouble that's brought me here now, I have information that this house is used by one of the worst receivers in London, and that a proper search would reveal a great many interesting things. That may be true or not. I shouldn't expect you to tell me if it were, and, so far as tonight goes, I don't want to know.

"I want you to understand this. I'm after men, not goods, tonight, and if you don't stand in my way you'll have nothing to fear from me."

Mr. Ormerod listened to this without interruption. He showed no sign of any feeling, unless he went a little paler, which was hard to say in that light. He answered quietly: "I'm not obstructing you at all. I only tell you that you are entirely mistaken. I am sure that you will find no one in the house except my daughter and myself, because there is no one here. If you would take my word for that, you would save time, during which the men you are seeking may be making good their escape. But if you are determined to search my house, with your fifty men"—he smiled slightly as he repeated the inspector's number—"how can I prevent it? I can only protest and submit.

"As to my own character, you will find, if you make proper inquiries, that I have held a position of trust with the Orient Shipping Line for over twenty years. You will also find that I have been the vicar's churchwarden at St. Peter's for about the same period, and that my reputation is such as to be a sufficient answer to the imputation that you have made.... At the same time, I am pleased to hear that, if you insist on searching the house, my property will at least be respected."

"Yes," the inspector answered dryly, "I thought you would."

He got up with the word, but he was inwardly somewhat uncomfortable. If the men he sought were not here, he was making a fool of himself, and losing time, which was even worse. He did not think that this man, whether or not he were in with Rafferty, would act quite as he did if he knew that the men would be found on the upper floors. But of course he might be going to say that they had got in without his knowledge—and it was barely possible that that was a true explanation. He had to take what comfort he could from that possibility, and from the thought that Mr. Morrison had given him the address.

Half an hour later he left the house in no very cheerful mood. He had searched it from roof to basement, and he had satisfied himself that he had wasted his time. It had been as Ormerod had told him at first. There was no one but himself and his daughter there. The inspector was certain that he had not overlooked any corner that could have harboured a cat.

Neither had he observed any article or accumulation of articles of a suspicious character. The house had, indeed, exposed an interior which equalled its exterior dullness and respectability. He was forced to the reluctant conclusion that Mr. Morrison had given him the wrong number. Had Mr. Morrison been fooled? If so, he had a comforting conviction that whoever was responsible for that audacity would have some trouble to come.

For the time, there seemed to be nothing to do but to set a watch on all the houses of the block. He knew that McClure was already attending to the routine work of circulating the necessary descriptions and information, and that inquiry was being made as to whether Miss Collingwood was in the safety of her own bed. Perhaps, he had better seek his also, for some much-needed sleep. Dull, but distinct, there came the sound of a shot interior of the adjoining house.

The inspector's whistle sounded shrilly darkened street, as he led the way next door.

CHAPTER XXXV.

FLEDA looked round the room, and at the girl upon whom she had been thrust so unceremoniously. A girl of about twenty-three. Perhaps rather less than that. A blonde girl, of the pleasant, ineffectual type. One of whom anyone would say that the brains were doubtful, but the character beyond suspicion. She seemed a little uncertain, a little shy, but without resentment of this unconventional intrusion. Certainly, she did not appear to regard it with any seriousness, or to have any sense of wrongdoing into which she was being drawn. Fleda wondered what explanation her father could have given. Later in the night, the girl would puzzle Inspector Cleveland in the same way, forcing him to the conclusion that she was either a consummate actress, or else, as he was more inclined to think (correctly) that she was innocent even of the knowledge of whatever evil might be active around her.

Fleda drew some confidence from a further reflection. The triviality of her attitude as she timidly offered her the resources of her own wardrobe and toilet-table, and contrived, rather self-consciously, to introduce the information that she had won a set of brushes at a local tennis tournament, showed clearly enough, not only that she was unaware of the circumstances which had brought her this unexpected guest, but that there was nothing in her experience to disquiet her mind with a premonition of resulting trouble.

In this atmosphere Fleda quickly lost her sense of restraint and danger, and, though she could not suppose that no precautions had been taken to prevent her leaving during the night, she would have been sleeping very quietly, with a carefree mind, had she been permitted to do so.

But when she was half-undressed, she noticed that there was no key in the lock, and said to Adeline: "Don't you ever lock the door?"

"No, I never thought of it. There's only Daddy and I in the house, after the woman goes home."

Just then there was a heavy foot on the landing, and the door opened, and Callaghan walked in without ceremony.

"You can't stay here," he said roughly. "I'll give you two minutes to get your things on, or pick them up, and if that isn't enough you'll have to leave them behind."

Fleda faced him with the determination born of an inward fear. "I shan't move again. I've had enough of it for one night, and I'm quite comfortable here."

"You won't, won't you? Do you reckon we can't haul you along, if you won't walk? You'll be out of this room in two minutes, either dead or alive, and I don't know that it matters much which. If that young Thornford's at the bottom of this, there's a bullet waiting for him, and if you want to go the same way you won't have to ask twice."

"What you need," Fleda replied, in the firmest voice she could manage, hoping that the sudden beating of her heart was not apparent in her manner, "is a good solicitor."

Callaghan stared, but made no audible reply, observing that she was resuming her cast-off clothes, and accepting that as a sign of the acquiescence which he required, though it was probably actuated by a quite different motive. She went on to improve the opportunity further: "Mr. Morrison wouldn't act for you in the ordinary way. It's not only that he's very particular who he takes on, it's the fact that he's acting for Mr. Thornford already. But I could get over that difficulty if I really tried, and if you came to him in the morning, and told him your trouble—"

Mr. Callaghan had listened to her to this point with such attention as the urgency of the moment permitted. He knew that there are attorneys in New York who have political or social "pulls" which may be of the utmost importance to the security of the criminal who will pay their very liberal fees. Certainly, such a friend in London would be very opportune now. But, when she mentioned seeing Mr. Morrison tomorrow, it brought to his mind the immanency of the threatening trouble with unendurable irritation. What was the good of tomorrow when the cops were in dozens around his doors?

"You're a bit late with that talk," he said roughly, "when that young devil has brought these cops nosing along the roof. Come on now. There's no time to lose. I don't mean them to find us here."

"I'll come with you, because a talk'll do us both good, but if you're thinking that Mr. Thornford's had anything to do with the police inquiring for us round here, if that's what they're really at, then you can guess again, for you're dead wrong. We don't want the police in on this deal any more than you do yourself; that is, if you're square with us. But if you said that Bletchworth's are at the bottom of it, I shouldn't say but you might be somewhere near the spot. That's why I'm trying to tell you the way out if it's not too late.

"You've got one of Bletchworth's clients here, and you've got one of their staff, and for all they know we might both want to be somewhere else, or even missing a meal, and if you think they're a firm to stand that without giving you a warm time it shows that you don't know them at all.

"You might get away with it, if you'd only got the police to think of, or if you'd quarrelled with all the crooks in London, but what you're doing is to bring them all on you at once from both sides.

"Mr. Morrison just telephones to Scotland Yard, and out come the police, and then he rings up a few of the big crooks that come to him when they get jammed, and the word goes round, and in a few hours there won't be a place high or low where you can lie up, from Buckingham Palace to a Limehouse slum."

As this speech proceeded they descended the remaining stairs, and crossing the hall with no better light than came from the street through a fanlight over the front door, entered a back room where the gas was lighted, and the remainder of the gang were gathered, with Basil in their midst, and Mr. Ormerod waiting, candle in hand again, in a nervous impatience for their appearance.

Callaghan said no more than, "Anyone'd think, hearing you talk, that— But we've no time for that now."

But there was something in his tone which gave her a comforting hope that her somewhat picturesque account of the activities and influence of the firm which had the benefit of her services had not been wasted upon him. It influenced the reassuring glance with which she answered the anxious questioning in Basil's eyes, and the light tone of her remark to him that it began to look as though they were going to have a bad night's sleep.

Basil saw that she had no wish to cause trouble, or even delay, and it was a decision of a very evident wisdom, for what could they have done against the five armed and lawless men, who were now regarding them with a savage suspicion, as the probable cause, direct or indirect, that the cops were upon their trail.

Mr. Ormerod led the way through a door that opened into the kitchen, and then to a little pantry upon its further side. This pantry had shelves around it, of which he lifted down from their supporting brackets those that crossed the narrow end wall which faced the door. Then he pressed a spring which the simple scroll-work of one of these brackets concealed, and the wall moved away. It was a door into the pantry of the next house.

"You go first, Devlin. Now, hurry along. No, Dancer, I go last. After you."

They were all through now, with Mr. Ormerod's candle in Callaghan's left hand. His right held a ready gun, and his eyes were on Dancer in a way which that gentleman found rather annoying.

The wall closed behind them, as Inspector Cleveland's heavy knocking sounded in Mr. Ormerod's ears. He hurried up to warn his daughter not to mention their unwelcome visitors, and to prepare himself to face the inspector as a man suddenly awakened from a peaceful sleep.

CHAPTER XXXVI.

DEVLIN, going ahead, flashed an electric torch cautiously round the kitchen into which they came. He kept the light low at first, not wishing to attract the attention of anyone who might be watching at the back of the house. But there was no danger of that. The windows were closed with heavy wooden shutters.

It was a commonplace, rather untidy kitchen, with the remains of a meal and two unwashed plates on the table, showing that the house had more legitimate occupants than the present intruders. It differed in no way from ten thousand other London kitchens in houses of similar type, unless it were that there was a wall-telephone beside the door, and these instruments are rarely installed in such kitchens. But an exploration of the rest of the house would have shown less usual features, excepting only in the attic-room where Mr. and Mrs. Catkin slept.

Mr. Catkin was a grocer by trade, an elderly man of quiet respectability, who owned a lock-up shop at the corner of Wilton Street. He paid no rent for his tenancy of the house, and he was never asked to make any reduction of the loaned capital which had started him in business ten years ago. But his occupation was limited to the kitchen and attic. The other rooms were locked, and it was understood that he was not under any obligation to give a burglar-alarm should he at any time be disturbed by noises in the night. He was to stay where he was.

Mrs. Catkin understood this as well as he, and when she heard steps on the roof, and a policeman's lantern was flashed into the attic, though she was a frightened woman, she did not wake her husband, nor give any evidence of consciousness herself, and as the signs and sounds of unusual activity increased during the next hour she went to sleep all the more.

Meanwhile, her kitchen, which was not very large, was occupied by seven people in various conditions of ill-temper, anxiety and suspicion, and all suffering from the lack of sleep. They were rather

166

thick on the ground in a literal as well as a figurative sense, for there were only two chairs. Callaghan had ordered Devlin to sit on the floor with his back to the door, so that no one should leave without his knowledge. He was not only thinking of Basil and Fleda, but of Dancer also, of whose loyalty he was less than sure even after the physical persuasion that he had applied. He sat down himself on one of the chairs, putting its back to the pantry door through which they had entered. Flipps took the other chair, possibly out of consideration for his wounded ear.

There was no chair for Fleda, for whom Basil cleared a space on the table, apologizing for its less than doubtful cleanliness.

"Never mind that," she replied. "It can't do it any harm now." She alluded, resignedly, to her dress, for which she had not anticipated any possible convalescence since it had slid down from the higher level of the hotel roof.

"Now, boys," Callaghan's voice, low but dominating, interrupted them, "we're quite safe here, if we keep dark and quiet. They seem to know the house we made for, though it's hard to tell how, for I'd kept the idea in my own mind till I gave the word to move, but they can search it from top to bottom now, and they'll never guess where we are. They'll think they were a bit late, and we gave them the slip at the street door. So quiet's the word, now, and when we know they're gone I'll have something to say."

It was dark in the shuttered kitchen, even when their eyes got used to the gloom, and the gang sat in an uneasy silence, with hands that had a tendency to feel for their pistol-butts, and ears alert for the faint sounds of movements in the next house, where Inspector Cleveland and his men were commencing their fruitless search.

Dancer, more than ever distrustful of their leader's capacity to bring them clear under these unfamiliar conditions, still harboured treachery in a frightened mind. He had a well-grounded fear that, if the gang came into armed conflict with the police, it would be very difficult for him to establish subsequently that he had been a dissenting party from any resulting violence, and there was in the hearts of all of them a terror not so much of the severity as of the inevitability of the English law. But his three companions were nearer than himself to the usual gangster pattern. Men of brutal rather than cunning minds, and content to rely upon their boss rather than concern themselves at the dilemma in which they lay. The heads of more than one nodded forward as the minutes passed.

But Callaghan did not nod. His mind worked with a savage activity, probing the position that he might have to face, the decisions which it might be necessary to make before the next day would be over.

Should he surrender if the police should find them here, or fight his way out, as he would have ordered without hesitation had he been in his own villa in Queens? Should he surrender, how serious would his position be? Considering that, since he came to London, he had done nothing—simply nothing at all! That was the exasperating fact. A mere attempt to establish a sound financial understanding with the police, and even that a project which had not matured! As for these two young fools, if it were their disappearance which had roused this midnight hunt—well, he might make some fairly good defence of that. At least, he could do so, if he should tell all the truth, to which, unfortunately, there was the one formidable objection that he did not want the police to see what the pocketbook held.

If they were the object of the search, everything might depend upon what they themselves would be prepared to say. The girl had already said, in the presence of a witness, that she was there of her own will. But would she say that it was of her own will that he had brought her into the next house? Having learnt the importance of preconstructing such positions with accuracy, he foresaw a possibility that might undo him. If, for the sake of a division of that deposited money, his captives might be indisposed to bear such witness against him as would place the police in control of the situation, they must be ready with some plausible explanation, such as would relieve them of the damaging suspicion that they were in actual league with his gang. That made it important that he should establish a prompt and friendly understanding, if it were still possible, He remembered Fleda's words on the stairs, as she had meant him to do.

Yet he hesitated, even then. There was so much of which he could not be quite sure. It was still a possibility that the police were not after him at all, and that he had blundered into a trap which was set for another prey. It was possible, too, that he had been actually betrayed by one or both of his captives, in which case he was viciously resolved that they should not escape alive. But his present position was one which, at the best, might be improved, and every chance should be tried. When he thought of all his possessions in the hotel suite; when he thought of the suave representative of the Cunard who would be calling there at 10:30 A.M., and who must be seen if he were to get away by Saturday. Smithers began to snore on the floor, and he reached out his foot to relieve his mind with a kick at the offender's ribs. As he did this, he became aware that Basil and

Fleda were whispering together. Perhaps if he could overhear what was said it would give him the guidance he sought.

There seemed to be a little difference between the pair at the moment, and this feeling may have assisted to raise their voices to the slight extent he desired though the implication of what he heard was, at first, rather difficult to determine

"Of course I didn't mean that," Fleda was saying soothingly. "I know you're good with water-bottles, and I expect you're absolutely splendid with chairs, but I think, all the same, you'd better leave this to me. You must see that your position's just a bit complicated."

"I suppose," he answered, "what you mean is that you want to play the Alice Brand stunt." The opportunity for quotation was irresistible even then:

> And if there's blood upon his hand,
> A spotless hand is mine.

Not that there's any blood on my hand, except Flipps's, and I don't think that counts. I shouldn't have minded if it had been a bit more."

"I wasn't thinking of Mr. Flipps's blood. I don't think that matters at all. It's the *aliases*. Having three a week, I mean. And besides that—"

The voice became too low to catch, and for the next five minutes Callaghan listened in vain to a conversation that did not slacken, but that was rarely audible. It seemed to be of an increasing concord as it proceeded, and only twice was Basil's voice raised enough to be heard, and then in no comprehensible way. Once he said, "Well, I don't much mind, so long as I'm not late seeing Ethel," and the other time he appeared to repeat something which had not been understood at the first whisper. He said, "Yes, grey squirrels. Can't you see what I mean?" And after a moment's pause, Fleda had replied, "Yes, I see. That's just it."

Suddenly he became aware that while he listened his mind had made itself up. Sounds had ceased from the other side of the pantry door. The police had gone entirely, or were searching a more distant part of Mr. Ormerod's residence. He flashed his torch on Fleda for a second, and as he did it a little rustle of paper caught his ear. He extinguished it again as he said, with a purposed loudness, so that all the gang might hear: "Miss Collingwood, I've been thinking over what you said on the stairs half an hour ago. If I put this matter in the hands of your firm, can you assure me that they'll arrange it so that we can get away by Saturday?"

"No," Fleda said boldly, "I can't promise anything. I can't even promise that Mr. Morrison'll take it on. But if he does, and you want to do anything by Saturday, he'll fix it up, if there's any way at all. If he won't take you on, or if he can't fix it the way you want, he'll tell you straight, and you'll be no worse off than you are now. Ask Rafferty, or any of the Bestwick lot. They'll tell you what his way is. I'll find out in three minutes, if you'd like to know."

"How?"

"Ring him up, of course. He's always on the line at Surbiton during the night."

"Very well. You can do that." He flashed the light on to the telephone as he spoke. As he did so he heard that little instant rustle of paper again. Fleda was saying: "I don't need the light. I know the number by heart."

Callaghan's torch ceased its search for the telephone directory, crossed the door, against which Devlin still sat, passed rapidly over the electric-light switch beside it, and went out.

Fleda was at the telephone now. The listening gang heard her ask for the number "Surbiton 073," and then, after an interval, "Yes, I'm Fleda Collingwood. No. I can't say where I am. It wouldn't be fair. Not till you've agreed. Yes, quite. He's with me here. Well, *here*. And, Mr. Callaghan…I want you to act for him. He's rather in a hole, but he's not sure how deep. I told him you'd get him out, if anyone could, and you'd say so if not, and he'd be no worse off than he is now. I think that's what he wants. By Saturday, if he can. At the Pelican in something under an hour? Yes, I should think that would do."

Suddenly, before she had actually put the receiver back on to its hook, the kitchen was flooded with light, and the next instant she turned towards the noise of two men who rolled on the floor. Silently, while she spoke, Callaghan had crossed to where he had seen the electric switch that was beside the jamb of the door, and, as he pressed it, he had seen the paper on Dancer's knee, and leapt upon him.

Now he had him by the wrists, and had thrown him backward. He was breathing heavily, but declined the help of the advancing gang. "No, leave him to me. Devlin, see what he's written there."

Devlin picked up the paper that had fallen from Dancer's hands, heedless of the man's incoherent protestations.

It was not a paper that could be easily explained away. It had occurred to a cunning and frightened mind that if he should be captured by the police, under whatever circumstances, it would be to his advantage if a letter should be discovered upon him offering to betray his companions and repudiating their works, which he could explain that he had been seeking an opportunity to deliver. If there should have been armed resistance, and the police had suffered casualties, it might save him from the hangman's rope.

Devlin stumbled a moment over displaced and disjointed sentences, for Dancer had had no practice in writing without a light, and had twice lost his place on the paper when he had been startled into hiding it by the sudden searchlight of Callaghan's torch. But he read enough, and the wretched man looked up at his fellow-gangsters and saw no mercy in the faces around him. If he could only get at his knife. And, then, incredibly, he was aware that Callaghan's grip had slackened, not the grip on the wrist which prevented him feeling for the knife, but on that of his pistol-hand. With a fierce and sudden jerk, he released the arm. In another second his hand was firm on the pistol-butt, and in a third he would have settled Callaghan for ever and been in a position to fire upward at the other three, under the protection of the dead body above him. But that second did not come.

As the pistol came clear, Callaghan caught the wrist again in an iron grip, and gave it a quick twist. The shot came, but the bullet went in under Dancer's chin, and through the back of his head, and slanted off to the wall along the red quarries below.

Dancer made no sound. He quivered and lay still.

Callaghan loosed his hand, in which the gun was still firmly gripped.

"You see that, boys," he said. "He shot himself with his own hand." His eyes, hard and challenging, stared at Fleda's bloodless face, and went on to Basil's with a merciless interrogation, both of himself and them.

Basil looked at the dead man. The outward damage had been mostly to the back of the head, which the floor concealed—only round it now was that red, widening patch. At that moment he saw enough of the way the master criminal treads to give him a lifetime's thought. But at the moment he felt faint, and then thought of Fleda's peril, and his courage rose. He saw what must be done. What did a thousand such as Dancer weigh in an opposite scale to her?

"Yes," he said steadily, "he shot himself. I saw that."

Fleda did not know until afterwards how frightened she really was. There was nothing strange to her mind in such incidents. For the last three years she had typed briefs. She had sat in Mr. Morri-

son's office taking down evidence, true or false, of very nauseating
kinds. She had shaken hands with a man who had used a carving-
knife upon his family in a wholesale way, and didn't feel sure
whether he minded, or whether it was right or wrong, but didn't remember very clearly what had started the row. But hearing is not
sight.

Still, her familiarity with criminal exigencies enabled her to
analyse the position in a way which Basil could not be expected to
equal.

"Yes," she echoed, "he shot himself," and was annoyed to think
that her voice shook, wondering if it sounded as strange to others as
to herself, as she added, "*You know we can't all do that.*"

Callaghan, quick as herself, saw that too. If the alliance with his
two captives had become a more precarious it had also become a
more desperately necessary thing. He looked round at the faces of
the three gangsters, and knew them ready for any order that he might
give. He heard the loud knocking that had commenced on the outer
door. There is no cruelty like that of fear. There was no mercy for
any except themselves in those men's eyes. He said: "Leave this to
me, boys." And then to Fleda, "That deal holds?"

"Yes," she said, and it seemed that something was planning outside herself, so that she only heard as the words came. "But if that's
the tale, you can't be too quick opening the door. You want to call in
the police as soon as you can." And then, "I'll go alone, if you like."
She felt that she might make a better first impression than these men
with the guns clutched in their nervous hands.

Devlin murmured at that. His thought was on the way back to
the roof, and a possible getaway, punctuated by backward shots at
any cops of a too-curious breed.

Callaghan thought he saw a better chance than that, which was
poor at the best. He saw also that Fleda was right—it must be taken
instantly, if at all.

"Go on," he said, "but he stays," looking at Basil as he spoke.
"You understand?"

She was not sure that she understood, but she saw well enough
that Basil's safety depended upon her success in finding a method
by which the gangsters would be content to surrender.

Basil, watching her go, was tempted to call to her not to come
back, but saw that such advice might increase her immediate peril.
He thought that the police would see to that.

CHAPTER XXXVII.

INSPECTOR CLEVELAND, knocking loudly at the silent door, and debating inwardly whether he would be justified in forcing an entrance, was relieved to see a light in the hall. He felt certain that the shot had been fired within that house, and that it was his duty to investigate it. He knew that he was dealing with a gang of alien criminals of a particularly lawless kind, and he had the disappearance of Basil and Fleda to investigate. Who knew what tragedy might be enacting in that silent house while he knocked at a closed door?

But he had already made an absolutely illegal search of a house in which he had found nothing to excuse his intrusion. He knew that he was pursuing a course of action which could only be justified, if at all, by its own results, and that he risked reprimand, if nothing worse. from his superiors, should he blunder further. He would do what he thought to be his duty, even at such a risk, but he much preferred that that door should be opened from the inside in the usual way.

Yet the fact that it was being so opened, and that the house continued silent except for the light footsteps that sounded along the hall, and the drawing of heavy bolts, raised a reasonable doubt as to whether he were not about to draw another disconcerting blank, which disposed him to a preliminary caution, very favourable to the purpose in Fleda's mind.

She opened the door a few inches, fearing that she would have to stem a crowd of policemen, impetuously waiting to rush into the premises, but door was thronged with dark official uniforms, with the helmeted heads of ordinary constables rising behind the little group of Inspector Cleveland's special service men, she was not confronted either by haste or pressure.

The inspector's light flashed over her for a moment before he spoke and, though her appearance alone at the door might be puzzling enough, what he saw convinced him that he had made no mistake in demanding entrance.

It was a shot in the dark, but one that hit the mark, when he asked, "Miss Collingwood?"

"Yes," she said, wondering that he should know her. "You are Inspector Cleveland?" and ended a similar wonder in his own mind by adding,

"I've seen you when you've called at Bletchworth's."

The inspector came to the point. "I want a man called Buddy Callaghan, and his gang. Are they here?"

If she denied it, he meant to search the house all the same, but he was puzzled as to what her relations with them could be that she should be opening the door thus, and he looked for guidance in her reply.

"Yes," she said, "but I want to talk to you before you come in. There's been a man killed."

"Thornford?"

"No. A man named Dancer. He shot himself."

"You must let me pass, Miss Collingwood, please."

"Inspector, she said resolutely, "there are four frightened men in the kitchen, and they've got guns. They've got Mr. Thornford there too. They'll surrender, all right, if you let me go back to them first, but if they start shooting—"

"If they do that, it's their lookout, and they'll end up where they belong."

"But they don't want to, only I've promised to explain first. If you'll promise to wait till Mr. Morrison gets here—he'll be here in about half an hour now."

"You're wrong about that, Miss Collingwood. He's at home at Surbiton."

"He's on the way in now."

"How do you know that?"

"I've just rung him up, and asked him to come straight in."

"He's coming here now?"

"Not here. To the Pelican. But we can phone them to send him on."

By this time, Fleda had stepped back, and allowed the inspector to enter the hall with several of his men. He said: "I'm sorry, Miss Collingwood, but I can't wait for him. If there's been a man killed, it's my duty to investigate it at once, quite apart from any other reason I have for wanting these men. Of course it would be better for them to surrender quietly. Much better for them."

"That's what I've told them."

"What influence have you with them?"

"I've promised that Mr. Morrison will act for them if they behave sensibly."

"Can you go back to them safely?"

"Yes. I think so. It might depend on what I say when I get there."

"I can't have you running any risks. I couldn't say more than that I'd give them five minutes to come out quietly, and give up their guns."

"If they give up their guns, will you wait till Mr. Morrison gets here before you make any arrests?"

"I shouldn't let any one leave the premises."

"They wouldn't expect that. They only want Mr. Morrison to talk it over with you first."

"Very well. You can promise that."

With some inward anxiety he watched her go back to the kitchen. If harm came to her, or if the delay had been used by the men to effect their escape, he would be open to blame from his superiors Worse than that, he might blame himself. Yet he thought it was the best way. He did not see how they could escape, his men being placed as they were. He knew that, if they should offer resistance, their position could not be rashly attacked. It would have been a matter of calling on them to surrender, and falling back from the first shots to concert some method of attack which would not needlessly imperil the lives of his own men.

Fleda came back almost at once.

"Mr. Callaghan says, if you'll come first, and tell him it's O.K., he'll tell the boys to give up their guns, if you won't try any third degree till Mr. Morrison's here."

"Gibbons," said the inspector, "if I'm not back inside five minutes, you carry on, as though I didn't exist. Miss Collingwood, you stay here."

He went down the passage, and entered the kitchen alone.

CHAPTER XXXVIII.

THE inspector looked round the kitchen, at Basil still leaning against the table, at the sullen, scowling gangsters, at the dead man on the floor.

"Mr. Callaghan," he said, "you've given me some trouble to-night. And it looks as though you've had some trouble here yourself too. I'm going to tell you plainly that I've a warrant for your arrest, though I've not much against the other men here, unless it's this on the floor. I've told Miss Collingood that if you all give up any weapons you have I shan't make any arrests till you've had a chance of talking it over with Mr. Morrison, and after that I'll hear what he's got to say. I don't promise more than that."

"That's O.K. with me," Callaghan said.

He put two pistols on the table. The others added theirs. The inspector called at the door: "Gibbons, come along."

He looked down at Mr. Dancer, unbeautiful in death, as he had been in life. He looked up at Basil.

"See this happen?" he asked.

Now, as a matter of fact, Basil hadn't. He might have his own opinion, but he had been obstructed by a limitation of vision, such as that alleged by Mr. Samuel Weller on a somewhat similar occasion when on Mrs. Bardell's stairs. His sight had been obstructed at the fatal moment by the breadth of Buddy Callaghan's back.

> I could not see the fight,
> For the smoke it lay so white.

Those were the lines that echoed in his mind. They had a particular appositeness, almost causing him to quote them to the inspector in reply. Only, they would mix themselves up with other quotations in an exasperating manner.

> I saw 'im lyin' dead,

With a bullet through 'is 'ead,
And that's being Mistress of the Sea.

It must be the lack of sleep, or the excitement, or something, but it is annoying when things get mixed up like that. Things that you really know quite well. He said: "Yes."

But the inspector noticed the hesitation. He was inclined to ask more, but he remembered the bargain he had made. It was not exactly a breach of that understanding to question Basil, but there might be no loss in delay. It might be better to talk to him alone.

He looked at the little pile of deadly weapons that Sergeant Gibbons was removing from the table, and he felt that things might have gone worse.

He looked at the deceased Dancer, and the thought repeated itself. Illogically, but no less actually, his midnight raid, with whatever incidental irregularities, had been justified by that opportune fatality.

And the man, with the pistol still gripped in his hand, did appear to have killed himself. Yes—appear. That was the word. He was too old in experience to be satisfied quickly by such appearances. But there would be several witnesses who would be likely to swear to the same tale, and, apart from that, his case against Callaghan depended upon the essential evidence that Morrison was to produce. Yes, it was well in every way to have Morrison here before he jumped down on either side of the wall.

He turned to speak to Basil again, and found that he was more agreeably occupied. Miss Collingwood had lost no time in returning to the kitchen. Basil was saying, "It's the grey squirrel stunt that'll pull it through, if anything will." And Fleda answered, looking at him with something approaching admiration in her eyes, "Yes, it's your idea if it comes off. I won't forget that."

Well, whatever they were talking about, they seemed happy enough. He judged that, if they had only been thrown together since yesterday afternoon, they must have made good use of their time. We know him to have been wrong by a good many hours, but, looking fairly at the whole position, we may agree that they had.

The inspector turned to a less pleasant but more professional observation of the defunct Dancer. There was no possible doubt that he was dead. He had better lie as he was till the police surgeon should arrive, which might be any moment now.

"Robb," he said, "just cover it over, and see that no one comes too near."

The gangster's body suffered the indignity of being covered with a very dirty kitchen table-cloth.

As the inspector gave this order, Mr. Morrison walked in.

He did not appear to look at anything, nor to exhibit any surprise at the tableau which met his eyes.

"I haven't been to the Pelican," he explained, "I thought it might save time if I drove this way first. I think, now I'm here, I'd better have a few words alone with Miss Collingwood, if you'll give us a room by ourselves, Inspector, for ten minutes."

"I'm afraid I can't do that, Mr. Morrison, unless I break in. Every room here is locked about three times, except the attic, and there's an old couple there who can't wake up enough to tell me anything more than that they're let off. Still, I don't know why I shouldn't have a look. It's not Number 36."

"Not Number 36?" Mr. Morrison stroked his head thoughtfully. "Oh, no, you mustn't, Inspector. Not tonight, anyhow. We'll talk about that in the morning, when I know more. Miss Collingwood, you'd better come and sit in my car. You seem to have been enjoying yourself since yesterday."

CHAPTER XXXIX.

IT was about twenty minutes later that Mr. Morrison returned with Fleda to the crowded kitchen. He was a man who liked to be sure of his facts, and to assimilate them without haste. At the end, he had said no more than, "Well, we must see what we can do," but Fleda, knowing his usual manner, was not dissatisfied.

"Inspector," he said, "I shall want a few words with Mr. Callaghan. I suppose you'll let him come out to my car?"

Inspector Cleveland looked doubtful, and the solicitor added: "You can put your men round it three deep, if you like. But I'll be responsible. We're not silly enough to do any running away, eh, Callaghan? We think we can get through rather better than that."

Callaghan agreed to that, feeling that there was hope in the tone of this solid, slow-moving man, whom the inspector treated with evident respect. The latter fact was capable, to his mind, of one explanation only. Mr. Morrison had a "pull." No, he certainly was not going to try running away, and without his gun too. He followed Mr. Morrison out into the street and the privacy of the empty car.

The conversation that followed need not be recorded fully. At the first, Callaghan talked, and the solicitor did not listen overintently. He let him talk himself out. Then he said: "You want to get back to New York. Ever want to come here again?"

Mr. Callaghan said no, with an expletive sincerity.

"We might manage that," the solicitor said slowly. "But there's one other thing I want to talk to you about first. It's about a pocketbook."

"We've fixed that up," Callaghan answered, not welcoming the introduction of the subject, though it did not surprise him. Doubtless they were coming to its contents, part of which must be surrendered as the solicitor's fee. Well, that couldn't be helped. He had plenty of dollars in New York. It was the getaway that mattered, at any cost. But he was not prepared for what followed.

"What I want to be clear on, before I talk to the inspector, is that we've been going under a mistake. Callaghan, *that pocketbook wasn't yours.*"

"Wasn't mine?" exclaimed the astonished gangster.

"I understand that you were robbed by Bolshie Joe, and that you got Rafferty to insist on your property being returned. Joe tells me that he saw you at the Pelican and gave you back a wallet containing twenty pounds. It's an important point, because the police have got copies of some of the papers that are in that pocketbook and they think they can link them up with an attempt at bribery which they're very anxious to prove. Callaghan, you're an English subject, aren't you? If you get convicted here, you won't be readmitted to the United States, however long you may have lived there. You'll never see Broadway again."

"You mean you want the lot, if you get me clear?"

"Callaghan, you're not as smart a man as I should have thought. I'll send you my bill when the time comes, and I'll trust you to pay. You won't make me come over to collect that. There might be another of your lot in trouble over here some day, and it would be just as well for him if I could remember putting paid to that bill. I want you to get it into your mind that that pocketbook isn't yours or mine, and if no one claims it at all, and this young Thornford finds it left in his pocket, it'll be no more than he deserves if it's got you back to your own roost.

"Now, you just go back to the inspector, and tell him it's his turn. Ask him to be good enough to step out here. I'm a bit too stiff to keep getting up and down those steps."

Mr. Callaghan went, with a mind which was sulky, and yet more hopeful than it had been previously. His experience of the methods of his adopted city led him to the conclusion that the higher the price the more probable it was that the deal would go through. Doing great injustice to a quite honest if very shrewd solicitor, he did not doubt that the bulk of the money would find a home in Bletchworth & Co.'s safe. But, he admitted to himself, it would be cheap at the price.

The inspector lost no time in going out to Mr. Morrison's car. Indeed, that gentleman, a slow thinker as we have noticed already, was hardly prepared for him when he arrived, but he knew that it was his turn to do the talking now, and he commenced accordingly.

"Inspector I've heard what Callaghan's got to say, and I know what you've got against him, besides this shooting tonight.

"I'm going to put my cards on the table, and it'll be up to you to decide—I suppose you don't want a permanent addition to the criminal population of London?"

"No, we don't. We mean to get them deported the first chance we get."

"Well, you're going the wrong way. Ever heard of the grey squirrels?"

"I heard of some about an hour ago. I don't know whether these are the same."

"Well, they are. It's young Thornford's idea, but it's quite sound, and it's worth your while to think of it now.

"They're American squirrels, and they seem quite popular in their own country, and don't do any harm worth a fuss. I believe you can see plenty of them there without going further than Central Park. But some one thought they'd look pretty here, and before you could count ten they were all over the country, and our own red squirrel's dying out, and they're smashing nests, and eating eggs and young birds, and gnawing trees, and making hell generally, and it's a case of shooting them as hard as you can, and even that doesn't make much difference, because they're breeding like rats.

"Now what you're trying to do is to plant these American gangsters here in the same way, and a grey squirrel's bad enough, but a gangster's worse. They'll teach our criminals their own ways, and you'll curse the day that you didn't listen to me. They seem to like them well enough in New York. I suppose it's something in the air. But they'd never suit us.

"I suppose you haven't thought that this Callaghan was born on this side, and if you convict him he'll be here for life, and you've got nothing against the others. You've got to wait for trouble first, and deport them after that, if you can.

"Now what I offer is that they'll all be out of this country in about forty-eight hours, and it'll be your fault if you ever let them land here again. You'll keep that warrant ready that you've got in your pocket now, and there'll be all the evidence you need in my safe. I'll tell Callaghan that, and he'll know what to expect. But they won't try to come back. They'll keep others away. Ever lived near any jackdaws?"

"No. Why?"

"Because I have, and it just came into my mind. There used to be hundreds in a park near where I lived years ago. They used to come into my pigeon-loft, stealing the corn. Do you know how I stopped that? Well, I didn't shoot, because some one told me a better dodge. I just caught one, and gave him the fright of his life, and then let him go free.

"He told the rest, and there was no more trouble with that corn."

"Yes. I see what you mean, and it sounds sense. They haven't been very happy here. But what about this dead man?"

"There'll be time for the inquest, without keeping them back for that. You can hold it this afternoon."

"I didn't mean that. I'm not satisfied as to how he died."

"You've got six witnesses. He shot himself through the head."

"Lying on the floor?"

"Well, why not?"

"Only that he wouldn't."

"That's argument, not proof. It's no value, if six people say that he did. Besides, there's a reason. He'd just been caught writing something that would have given them all away."

"That was something like what I thought."

"Well, he's no loss. And, if he didn't shoot himself, you'll have to get up early to prove who did. Suppose you arrest Callaghan for that, and I get him off, as I probably should, where would you be then? Let sleeping dogs lie. Or why worry them to bite, when they'll slink off if you give them a chance?"

The inspector wavered. "You'd give me your word that they'd leave by Saturday?"

"If they're not gone by then, you can arrest Callaghan on Sunday morning, and I'll promise you he won't get less than two years."

"Then you've got the evidence?"

"I don't say that."

"No, but that's understood. I suppose that pocketbook—"

"Callaghan will deny that it was his property."

"And all the money?"

"He will deny that it was his. The amount it contained will be evidence that he is telling the truth. Any jury would see that. What I say is that I will find you the evidence you require if he should venture to land again. If he does that I shan't be acting for him."

"Yes, I see. I shall have to report this, Mr. Morrison. I'll let you know during the morning. I expect it'll have to come out the way you want. What about these men in the meantime?"

"I'll be responsible for them so far as that they'll be at the inquest this afternoon."

"That'll do for me."

"Then tell Callaghan to have a word with me first, and after that he'll be glad to get back to his hotel. And please tell Miss Collingwood that I'm waiting to drive her home. She won't want to be seen in the streets now it's getting light. Not in the state she's in."

CHAPTER XL.

AT half-past ten on Thursday morning, Basil was on the way to visit his sister-in-law. He sat yawning irrepressibly in the bus, but with a mind in the pleasant state of ease which is only experienced by those who have paid their legal fares, and looking forward with an unholy excitement to the expression which would appear on Devereux's face when he should tell him the news. For he had decided to stay to lunch. He had not only recovered the key and banknotes from beneath his bedroom carpet, he had been to the Safe Deposit, in the company of Mr. Peters, and withdrawn the pocketbook. Under a bargain previously made with Mr. Morrison he had removed £4,500 from its contents, which sum was now securely buttoned in his hip-pocket, to be exhibited at the right moment, after Devereaux had exhausted his expressions of incredulity. The pocketbook itself, with its remaining contents, he had handed over to Mr. Peters. This and the papers were to remain deposited with Mr. Morrison. The second five hundred-pound note was his fee for professional services rendered to Mr. Basil Thornford. Mr. Callaghan was destined to receive a separate account. Bletchworth & Co. might be a very honest but it was not a very cheap firm.

Still, Basil did not complain. He felt it to be much more satisfactory to be the one who paid £500 as a commission on the retention of £5,000, than to receive the smaller sum for the recovery of the larger. It was a case emphatically where it was more blessed to give than to receive.

For that the £5,000 was his property was already a settled thing. Mr. Morrison, feeling that it was too late to go home, had gone on to his office, after he had deposited Fleda at her own gate, and Scotland Yard knows no night.

At 8:45 A.M., after breakfasting comfortably at his club, Mr. Morrison had been able to ring up Mr. Buddy Callaghan, and tell him that, in his own language, it was all O.K. He, and his three companions, would be required to attend the inquest on Mr. Dancer's damaged remains at 3:00 P.M., and would then be free—free, that is, on condition that they would leave the country by Saturday, and free only until that day.

Mr. Callaghan had heard this news with a very natural pleasure, but he was one who overlooked little, and he inquired whether there were any danger from the coroner's jury. He had just been holding an inquest of his own into his remaining financial resources and their condition was little better than that of the unlamented Dancer. If it were a case of squaring the jury, he wouldn't have been the man to object, understanding business as he did, but it simply couldn't be done.

Mr. Morrison had assured him not merely that it would be unnecessary, but that, if he were still seeking a course which would make England his permanent home, he couldn't easily think of anything better than that. As a fact, no verdict might be rendered. The coroner, after hearing their evidence, would probably adjourn the inquest for the formal attendance of the police surgeon who had first inspected the body, and who would be unable to be present this afternoon. But he would tell them that their further evidence would not be required.

It was after this conversation that Mr. Callaghan returned to the table round which were seated Devlin, Smithers, and the ear-damaged Flipps, each with a little pile of paper money before him. Unfortunately for them, it was an accented adjective. They were very little piles.

"Boys," he said, "if it's the stokehole, we've got to go." If they had needed any conviction on that point they would have found it in the news he gave. They were not too innocent to appreciate the significance of that anticipated adjournment. If they delayed to leave, who could say what the evidence of the police surgeon might suggest? But it was not that thought alone which urged them to flight, so that Saturday seemed too far. In a country where you can neither come to a gentlemanly understanding with the police nor arrange a jury's verdict beforehand, how can any man feel secure? It was a nightmare land, from which they could only hope that a kindly heaven would allow them to wake again in the security of a Broadway speakeasy.

So they sat there waiting, in a financial anxiety such as they had not known since they had graduated in their profession, for Mr. Callaghan had asked for his bill. He had asked for it to be made up to Saturday morning in advance, so that he should know how much would be left when the representative of the shipping company should arrive to arrange their passage. And when it came it was a very doleful document.

It was not merely that it was more than he had anticipated. Hotel bills always are, and we all expect them to be so. But it was more—much more—in excess of his estimate than he had expected it to be. It included the repair of a telephone, and the replacement of a water-bottle, and a chair, *en suite*, and the value of these articles had been estimated in a liberal mind. Indeed, everything had. Mr. Callaghan had become used to hotel bills of a princely size, and to settling them in a princely way. But this was an even princelier bill than he was accustomed to receive, and.... But he had his own pride, and his own code.

"Boys," he said, "throw it in. What's ten days? We'll be home by then, and if we ever come here again...." There was no need to complete the sentence. They were all of one mind on that point. And, besides, they knew it was largely their own fault. Dancer was known to have more money in hand then the rest of them had produced collectively, and it had not been found among his effects. It must be in the hands of the police now, and much chance there was that they would ever see it again. Talk about butter in a dog's mouth! And there was the diamond ring on his hand too, which they might have taken any time for twenty minutes before the inspector walked in.

Well, it was too late to regret. And the money that they put up now was barely enough for the hotel bill. They must make a collection of their own jewellery; and though they knew that diamonds were down, and some of them had had bitter experience of the ghastly difference between the prices which are paid to obsequious jewellers and those that are given by them in less obsequious moods, they had a well-founded confidence that they could raise sufficient to float themselves across the Atlantic with the preliminary and incidental expenses attached thereto. But it must be steerage for them. There was not even time to cable for funds in this grotesque extremity. Buddy Callaghan, one of the uncrowned kings of New York, must travel steerage in the *Olympic*! Could anything beat that? The absurdity of the idea almost neutralizes its tragic side. Even at this moment of disordered flight they felt instinctively that wherever Buddy Callaghan travelled would be the aristocratic end of the boat. Really, it was their own fault. They saw that clearly enough. It all came from descending into effete and barbarous lands. There was not a gangster in Chicago, not a hijacker on the Canadian border, not a bootlegger on the Pacific coast, but would hear the news, and take warning to confine his future wanderings within civilized bounds.

The Cunard Company does not usually collect steerage passengers from the Pelican, and the ritual which precedes their departure differs in important particulars from that to which first-class passengers must conform, but the gentleman who called upon them while Basil's bus was proceeding westward, and Fleda, if the truth must be told, was ingloriously asleep in bed, did not seem surprised when Mr. Callaghan, with his cigar cocked at its jauntiest angle, informed him that they were going back on the cheap.

He did not even infer this to mean that they would be content with second-class accommodation, but had, surprisingly enough, all the necessary forms for steerage passengers in the recesses of his portfolio. Neither did he make any difficulty about the shortness of time for these preliminaries. The fact was that Mr. Morrison had had a few words with him on the telephone an hour ago, and after that he had rung up Scotland Yard and received the assurances that he required. The Cunard Company very naturally wished to be sure that it would not have to bring the gentleman back. At least, not at its own expense, Reassured as to that risk, it was quite willing to oblige the Metropolitan Police in any reasonable way.

Would it do if the passage-money were paid tomorrow? Yes, even that would present no difficulty. A deposit, however small—Buddy Callaghan, who had settled the hotel bill a few minutes earlier, handed over his last two pounds. Till they'd raised something on the little collection of rings and tie-pins which was now in Mr. Devlin's custody they wouldn't even be able to get a drink. Again, can you beat that?

CHAPTER XLI.

IT was 5:00 P.M. on Thursday afternoon when Miss Fleda Collingwood waked sufficiently to look at her watch, and after that she sat up with some celerity.

She had received permission, in the course of a very interesting conversation with Mr. Morrison, when he had been driving her home that morning, to delay her return to the office until after lunch, and the understanding that she should do so at that hour had been rather for the furtherance of her own plans than for the benefit of Bletchworth & Co.

Indeed, as a result of that conversation, Mr. Morrison had already informed Miss Simpson of impending changes which would bring her into more direct relations with himself, and entail the engagement of an assistant typist in her own room. Such was one only of the bewilderingly innumerable consequences following the agile movement of the digits of Bolshie Joe which had removed Basil's wallet from its natural home less than a week earlier.

But she found little consolation in the recollection that it was for her benefit rather than that of her employers that she was to have been awake at midday. She had put the question to Mr. Morrison, as a matter of some abstract interest, whether the absurd proposition that she should have married and departed from her native land by midday on Saturday could be dismissed as a legal impossibility, or whether she must decline it on its own merits, and she had received a reply that, though the time was short, it was not beyond the legal knowledge and resources of the firm to arrange it. Mr. Morrison had anticipated that the position in regard to the money would resolve itself during the morning, and had told her that if she were still of the same mind after some hours' sleep (she had noticed, with an excusable irritation, that he had ignored her explicit statement of what her mind was at that time) she had better come and talk it over with him at 2:30, when he would have a short time to spare. Doubtless, when the hour arrived, and she didn't, he would have concluded that

188

she had changed her mind, and probably, if she should announce in the morning that she wished to carry the project through, he would tell her that it was now impossible owing to the half-day she had wasted. What a nuisance Mary Daffern was! If she hadn't sat on the bed talking for nearly two hours this morning before she was obliged to clear out for her own office she would have been awake long before this.

With the illogical obstinacy of her kind, her inclination to carry through the idea increased with the thought that it might be no longer possible. Anyhow, Basil shouldn't say it was her fault, because she couldn't keep an appointment. In a space of time too short to mention, because it is always useless to record the incredible, a young lady in her pyjamas was through to Mr. Morrison's office.

Mr. Morrison said, if she really meant it, there was still time.

He mentioned that Mr. Thornford had been with him that afternoon, and his intentions, seemed clear.

He asked whether she had received a letter from his firm which had been posted earlier in the day.

She admitted that she had not yet been downstairs.

He said, well, it was nothing to worry about. As to her failure to keep the appointment this afternoon, it had not really mattered at all. Mr. Thornford had been carrying on at express speed. He believed he was on his way to see her now, or very soon would be. He had some documents for her to sign.

Fleda rang off, and decided that she had better dress.

As she did this, she had a change of mood. Her occupation naturally led her to think of clothes. She was aware of a bewilderingly numerous list of articles that she would require, if she were to have any pleasure in a first-class ticket to New York, or anywhere else. The actual time it would take to purchase them was a prohibitive thought. It would require every moment that remained, without twenty minutes to spare even for the conventional detail of a marriage ceremony. She was aware of Basil's idea that he might enlist the assistance of his brother's wife, but it did not appeal to her. Not in the least. It only showed what a hopeless fool Basil could be.

Besides, there was the expense. She did not doubt that he would hand over the cash with a free hand, but that was another idea that she did not like. She had an old-fashioned opinion that a girl should provide her own clothes on these occasions. She had twenty-seven pounds in the Post Office Savings Bank, but she thought uncertainly that it took two or three days to draw it out. Anyway, it wouldn't go far. She had a rather larger sum invested in a more permanent form.

She must have time to get that. She saw Basil's idea at last in its full absurdity. She would talk sense to him when he arrived.

She looked at the dress she had worn yesterday, and her resolution hardened. However few she had had before, she had one less now. What a sight she must have been!

She was in no very good temper when she went into the dining-room and found Mr. Morrison's letter on the table. She opened it with no anticipation of its importance, and read this:

DEAR MISS COLLINGWOOD,

Re Thornford.

We have received a fee of £500 for our services in this matter, and, in accordance with our usual practice, we are sending you £50, being the 10 percent commission allowed for the introduction of business of this character.

Re Callaghan.

We have also to thank you for the introduction of this client. We have not yet rendered his account, but as we understand that you may be severing your connection with us, we are adding a sum of £50 under this heading to the cheque which we enclose herewith.

Yours faithfully,

BLETCHWORTH & CO., C.M.M.

Miss Collingwood considered this letter in silence for some moments. She looked meditatively at the blue slip of paper which represented £100. You could do a good deal with that. Especially now that the sales were on. She looked at the time, and dashed at the telephone almost as impetuously as she had done half an hour earlier.

"Mary," she said, "you'd better know before you leave that you won't be at the office tomorrow. You'd better get the day off, or else you'll be too ill to go. It's no use asking why now. I'll tell you when you get home. For one thing, you'll be buying me a new hat."

ABOUT THE AUTHOR

SYDNEY FOWLER WRIGHT (1874-1965) penned over seventy volumes of science fiction, fantasy, classic mysteries, historical novels, poetry, and non-fiction, many of them being published by the Borgo Press Imprint of Wildside Press.

www.ingramcontent.com/pod-product-compliance
Lightning Source LLC
Chambersburg PA
CBHW032010240626
47153CB00003B/1191